L. A. F

FIRE & ICE

THE FLAME PRINCESS

Cover art by Asqa

Heading art by Canva.com

Editing done by Daniela Ferna and Gennifer Ulmen

ISBN: 979-8-89074-849-2

For my readers who are still finding their way

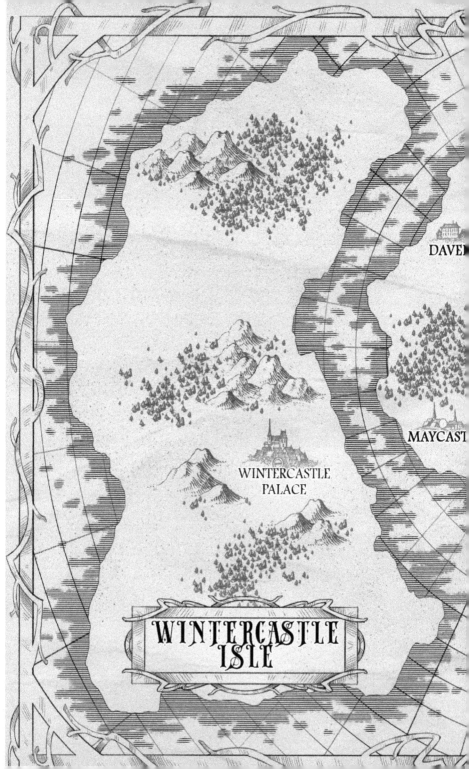

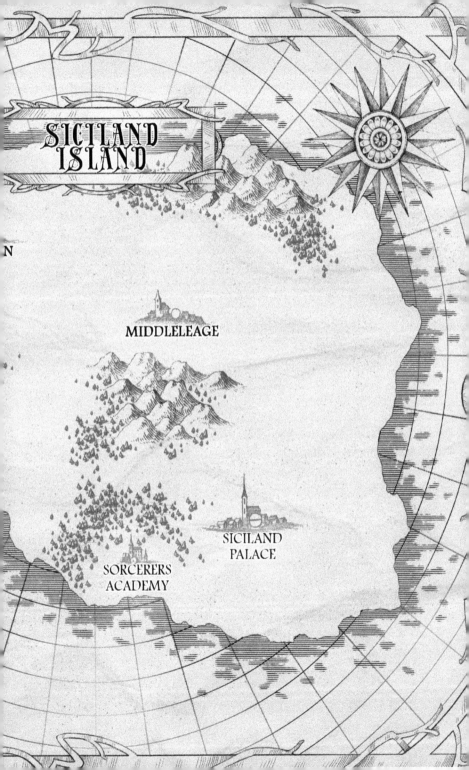

QUEEN OF FLAMES AND ICE

AND ICE

BOOK 1

PROLOGUE

WAR OF FANGS

I t was a war of fangs and fuel. Vira's eyelids weighed heavily as she ran around the battlefield. Yet another soulless vampire hit the ground.

"I'll get him this time," Jayden, the sorcerer of fire, said just as he cast a stroke of fire onto the headless body.

Perhaps he could tell how mortified Vira was of fire, even if she had been the sorcerer of flames. There was almost no time to think before the next headless body hit the floor. Vira casted her flame onto the chest as she watched it spread to the rest of the body and grow into a wildfire. A certain level of post traumatic stress occurred within her during the war. Even though the blood sucking, murderous vampires were the enemies, it was like Vira could see the scene of her mother being murdered by the fire that had no tame nor mercy.

Her mother's job as a circus performer had always seemed phenomenal to Vira when she would visit the shows, watching her juggle fire sticks wearing the most beautiful, dazzling leotard. That was, until one day a man covered her little eyes and carried her outside the tent. It was out of luck that Vira's vision was blocked at the time by a tall man who sat down in front of her at the perfect time. All she could hear were the screaming cries of the audience. Such an elementary mind couldn't comprehend at the time what it was really like to lose a parent and to only be left with the stepfather, the ruler of Siciland. Perhaps the pain grew only greater as she got older, and now that she was twenty three, there hadn't been a day that went by where she wouldn't kill to at least remember her mother as more than a blurred image.

It had been ironic that her chosen power was to be the sorcerer of flames. It was a common backstory for all of them, though. Vira's closest friend, Altha, had been the sorcerer of healing, and her parents had owned the Maycaster Clinic before a deadly car crash claimed the lives of them both.

"Are you okay?" Jayden tapped her shoulder and asked.

Vira literally shook herself out of the post traumatic trance. "Yes, I…" She couldn't find the words.

"Look, just do what I do and pretend like it's a game," he said as he began to run around the field, shooting the ground playfully with his fire as if it were a joke.

Vira let out a fake laugh, but shivered in fear.

Yeah, only this isn't a game for me, she thought.

But she still managed to pull her shoulders back and walk the field, casting fire on each vampire as they dropped. She developed a coping strategy: she never looked directly at them as she set them on fire.

Her pain bargained on the fact that there were more vampires dying than werewolves, which meant her side was winning. Perhaps the vampires knew about the werewolves when they came to invade, but had no clue the sorcerers even existed, which was, ultimately, the reason why it had looked the way of defeat.

One could say that the werewolves were to blame for the mess when one of them mistook a vampire tourist for a spy and ate him. This, ultimately, led to an invasion by the vampires as a way of striking back. Only the love between Altha and Zereck, a werewolf, had caused the sorcerers to step in. When Altha joined, they gave her her powers back, which had been taken away due to the forbidden romance. Vira knew they'd need Altha at some point and had come to terms with her value; this war just so happened to prove that value after all.

"Vira!" a high-pitched voice yelled.

Vira turned her head to the side, seeing that it was Altha calling her.

Altha had a look of terror on her face as she motioned to the opposite direction.

When Vira looked the way of the motion, she realized someone had finally come after her. Her mind was mixed between the surprise that it had taken this long for a vampire to come after her and the fear of a sudden death.

She froze as fear took over her body. She looked down towards her shaking hands, then turned her head back up at the male vampire running towards her. He was still way away, but every second went by quickly and more of his fine details became clear to the eye, which meant death would arrive any second. His face was sculpted and Vira couldn't decide whether his skin was pale tinted white or gray. Perhaps both. She wondered for a second if the collar on his white dress-like shirt was up on purpose. None of that mattered though. She was accepting death at that point.

Except that, at the last second, she decided not to give into that delusion. She balled up just one of her fists and acted as if she was throwing a ball, watching the flame roll from her palm to her extended middle and ring fingertips sending it flying into the direction of the enemy. When the flame hit his chest, Vira was almost startled as she realized the vampire wasn't caught on fire but instead was thrown up in the air, almost fifty feet up. Even a shadow was cast on the ground as he flew over the sun. Up until now, Vira hadn't killed anyone. She had only finished the job.

Vira held her breath as Altha walked over to her, setting her healing hand onto her shoulder in encouragement. They both stared up at the flying vampire until they lost sight of him. He must have gone into the ocean and drowned. Or maybe a shark finished the job. Or maybe he hit his head brutally on a sea rock, or the shallow ocean floor.

Whatever just happened, he has to be dead now, Vira thought.

Regardless, Vira turned to Altha and both shared a smile of accomplishment..

Vira walked away, making her way over to the ground to make sure there weren't any more vampires that needed to be set on fire. For the most part, it looked like Jayden did the job. He obviously enjoyed it a lot more than she did, which she was also fine with.

Standing by the bodies was her step father talking to the Alpha. They seemed to be in deep conversation, but Vira needed to know what would happen next in terms of the relationship between the sorcerers and the werewolves.

"Elvira." Her step father lit at seeing her as the last vampire hit the floor, courtesy of what looked like Zereck, Altha's boyfriend in wolf form.

"Hi, Father," Vira answered.

"I'll leave the two of you alone," the Alpha said. "Great game."

"Clearly," her step father answered with a smile as he walked away.

"Looks like we did good," Vira stated

"We did, we sure did." He nodded. "We need the wolves now."

"Yeah, so," Vira exhaled. "You guys are good to let Altha and Zereck be together?"

Altha meant a lot to Vira, and she appreciated the war bringing them together and breaking the forbiddenness of their relationship.

"There's going to be a meeting soon," he answered. "About ongoing plans."

Another meeting that Vira had no interest in going to, which was nothing new. She knew right away she wouldn't attend, especially since she knew the outcome of the meeting, which would be letting the two see each other again and giving Altha back her powers for good. Everything would work out for them they would have the happily ever after Altha craved all this time.

Good for her, Vira thought.

"You ought to go tell them," he suggested.

Vira exhaled, "Sure."

She walked away, seeing that Altha was talking to one of Zereck's brothers. She then looked around for Zereck, seeing him turn back into human form and approach Altha.

Altha eyed Vira when it became clear she was coming her way. However, Vira stopped quickly when she noticed Altha looking over at Jayden with a look of defeat on her face. The look of defeat came from the fact that he was now holding hands with one of the other sorcerers who joined the fight, Ezri. She was one of Altha's best friends. It was obvious to Vira that Altha wanted her and Jayden together because they were both sorcerers who played with fire and had the same hair color, so she assumed it would work out immediately so Vira could have her happily ever after, and Altha wouldn't feel guilty over making everyone go through literal war over her.

Vira knew one thing Altha didn't: she didn't care for a relationship set up by someone other than herself. Not that Vira was ungrateful towards Altha's attempt, but it just didn't work. It wasn't worth the trouble, either. Jayden was an attractive young man, but Vira knew he wasn't the one for her just by talking to him. He didn't excite her when he was near, and he didn't have nearly as much in common with Vira as Altha had anticipated. Vira believed she needed an opposite, someone who could balance her out.

However, this wasn't about Vira and she knew it. It was about Altha and the strained relationship between the sorcerers and the wolves now coming together firmly.

Vira walked over to give Altha and Zereck the good news, but she figured immediately after, she'd leave and head back to the palace to get out of her messy dress and leave the scene in general. It was all getting to be too much for her with the fire that brought flashbacks and the love that brought Vira's heart into an ache, wishing she had someone who'd turn her life into a fairy tale.

POST-WAR

The cold water felt indulgent against Vira's warm skin. The fire that flowed through her veins caused her desire for chilling showers, as it had been the utmost relief of the heat, even if she had gotten used to it by now.

The battle from the night prior put her deep in a rut. By the time she had made it back to the palace, the bottom trim of her gown was soaked in dirt and the tears were wider than she anticipated. She knew better than to bring her tiara to the war, as it would without a doubt have been lost somewhere in the mess.

It had only been her crown that made her feel like a princess. When she looked into the mirror, she would often see her own mother, especially when she would look into her own eyes. Her mother knew better than to base importance upon hierarchy status, which had been ironic that she ended up marrying the ruler of Siciland. And now, Vira was stuck with him, a man who was supposedly her family and her dad, but it still felt some days that she didn't know him well enough, or more so that she hadn't belonged to him in any way.

It was a common feeling for Vira to feel that she didn't belong. She would always guess if her true destiny had been the life that stood before her, but it was a tough thought most days.

At least when she had stepped out of the shower drying her hair, she felt the joy of utter relief. One, for washing the overheatedness out of her system and two, because the war was finally over. The war between the sorcerers and the werewolves had caused some backlash to her and the physical war between the two against the vampires really taught them something about the island as a whole, which had ended in bringing them closer together.

Now, the only issue had been the ongoing, which was staying a secret from the mortals. It would be a dangerous game if they found out about the immortals, but not too dangerous, as the immortals could easily defeat almost anyone who came their way. But still, war was of no interest to them after the previous events.

The palace was filled with sorcerers with the exception of the guards and servants who had been sworn into secrecy. The hierarchy was set for the sorcerers to work under the ruler, gaining their power that way. The wolves were directly under them, acting as soldiers if an invasion occurred or any other threats were present.

Vira wrapped her hair in a towel and tied herself in a plush, black robe after getting out of the shower. It would take no longer than minutes to dry her fine, deep wine colored hair. It had been a blessing and a pain at the same time. She scrunched her hair, wringing it out with the towel and tossed it in the hamper. She slipped on silk panties, then a lace bra to match before she headed into her room. A gentle knock sounded on her door.

"Hello," an elderly woman's voice said. "I'm here for your gown."

The dress Vira had almost destroyed during the war had been slumped over on the vanity stool. She had been surprised her father allowed even a speck of dirt in her room.

"Yes." Vira tightened her robe. "I'll be right there."

So she picked up the dress and stuck it in a tote that sat by the vanity. She cracked the door open and handed it to the woman, who she recognized to be the tailor.

The tailor took the bag, then did what Vira had hoped she wouldn't. She took the dress out of the bag and let it fall all the way open.

"My, my," she shook her head dramatically. "Look at all this dirt."

"I know, I'm alright though, no worries," Vira dismissed her, trying to close her door again and go back inside her room.

"No really, I'm going to have to spend a lot of time on this," she gasped as she said.

"Alright." Vira awkwardly giggled.

The tailor looked up at Vira with pursed lips and said, "Now I'm surprised your father even so much as allowed this mess in your room. I'll get right to it."

Finally, Vira thought as she gave the woman a friendly nod, then headed back into her room before locking it shut.

Vira adored her dresses, but she hadn't felt the need to abide by the rules and regulations that came with them. Despite their beauty, they became repetitive after a while. They were all a deep red, complimenting her long, voluminous hair. The detailing shone gold especially when brought into the light, which hadn't been often at the palace. It was like the lights didn't work all the way, or that they hadn't cared to invest in proper maintenance. But it gave off an elegant atmosphere, the way most of the rooms were naturally dim, and the lighter rooms had more of an off white lighting.

Vira opened up her closet, annoyed at the redundancy of wearing the gowns. Her eyes settled on a ball gown she normally favored, as it had only gone to her ankles and the straps were spaghetti style. Especially after the heat she had faced, being even more overheated was something she had no interest in going anywhere near. Since she had become the sorcerer of flames, it was a fret to be overheated, which seemed one of the many problems that came with her power.

The first dinner since the war would be on this night. It wasn't often that she'd get to see her stepfather in a better mood. Since the war had started with the werewolves, Vira fretted even just talking to him. Mainly because regardless of the topic, he'd find a way to lead a tangent about how much he disliked the wolf shifters. It was like she lost her last family member to a war, even if only mentally

This day, however, a new chance would arise to rekindle her relationship with her stepfather. Perhaps this recent event that made the island stronger would lighten him up to the point he'd finally ask her how she was doing. It wasn't often she felt sincerely cared about even in her own palace at least by him. But the dinner was something she immensely looked forward to.

THE LAST VAMPIRE

Vira had finally gotten around to making her bed. She felt the sudden urge to walk to the flower garden in the courtyard. It was often considered a normal practice for her after something prompted, like when she'd needed calming down or cheering up.

Vira patted the top of her pillow, smoothing out the last wrinkle, then picked up her tiara from the night stand. She bent down in front of the vanity mirror to fasten it on top of her head.

Finally, Vira left her room for the first time that day. The halls were rather busy. The servants were making their rounds as they held clear bags of trash over their shoulders on their way to the dumpsters. However, there had still been only a small presence of commotion in the hallways, as it had always been. Some of the guards had also been circling around the halls.

"Hello, Ward," she waved to one she happened to pass in the hallway.

Ward gave her a slight smile and a friendly nod while looking up at her as they passed each other.

Vira had walked past several more guards as she walked the halls of the palace, but it had always been hard to tell who was who, by the way the guards had been dressing. The uniform, a beige and white dressing with the bulky armor on the sides joined with the tall hat on their heads where the thick black strap covered most of the second half of their faces made it impossible to see their eyes or the shape of their faces most of the time. The few times Vira was able to reference a guard by their name would be after reading the cursive engraved name tag on them. Many guards Vira had passed she greeted only with a friendly smile and a wave.

As Vira opened the door to the courtyard, the smell of flowers blew off extra aroma as the breeze blew subtly. Perhaps the garden had been redone since the war already. Something seemed different about it. The flowers seemed more vibrant, more coordinated. The pastels of the beige, blood red and white mixed with deep pink complimented each other beautifully.

She stepped closer, admiring them. A small mist flew off them that sparkled as it blew away. Vira cocked her head in confusion. Normally, flowers wouldn't do that. But then she realized they had been put in place of the other flowers for the healer, Altha. Altha's healing powers centered around using these flowers to naturally heal people. Only, it hadn't been natural, and it was more so that the flowerers were her sorcery. It hadn't come from within, like Vira's. But it had seemed the flower garden was to keep the flowers growing to allow an unlimited supply of healing.

Vira smiled at them, taking in their beauty. But then she realized she was faking it. The smile, the admiration, everything. They were beautiful, but some level of Vira had still been filled with envy when it came to her best friend. Altha had it all. The healing power, the hero status, and now, her love life was enchanted. The war secured all of that for her. But Vira only felt mismatched to everything in her life.

Vira clenched her fists with thoughts about how upset she had been with everything. The jealousy, the fact that she couldn't stand her own power most of the time, the fact that she felt no love. But more than any of those things, the fact that her own mother died topped it all. All Vira wanted was her mother back. It seemed as though that would fix everything. But that wasn't possible. Being in her early twenties was scary, and growing apart from everything she had ever found comfort in and loved was painful. Sometimes it felt that somehow she wouldn't get through it.

Vira's heart skipped when she realized she had balled up her fists too tight and for way too long. Her palms started to warm and the fire had already started to travel through her veins right up her right arm, the one that she had squeezed the tightest. Her left hand grabbed her right arm as she tried to control it. She was in a flower garden. She knew she would be hated if she ruined it with her flames, which would add onto the reasons she ultimately disliked herself. But she huffed in panic as the fire came up too fast.

Vira unclenched her fists involuntarily. She attempted to aim it towards the ground, but it had no use. The flame rolled off the tips of her fingers. Her heart stopped as the flame flew, nearly hitting the flowery part of the garden, but hitting the back wall instead.

Vira held her hand over her chest in relief as her heart still pounded with the thrill. Luckily, it hadn't set anything on fire. Another thing she hated was her uncontrollable power. It was at times like she was mostly upset with herself, even if she knew that anyone would have a tough time with the flames if they had the burden of the power.

In the first week of Vira's sorcerer life, she had accidentally burned one of the servants after he had only asked if she'd like her coat hung up. When he attempted to take it off, she had unintentionally struck a flame to his chest simply because she got startled by his sudden closeness to her.

It had been clear to Vira that it would do good to her to take a break from the garden, at least for the rest of the day. She walked out the clear glass door that led to the outside.

The sound of water floating down the stream had calmed her down as she got closer, then stood next to it, yards away from the palace. The stream flowed down the path and, every so often, a small bubbling sound arose right before a Koi fish could come up to the water's surface. The beautiful border of multicolored rocks left helped easing her mind even more. She took a deep breath, allowing her heart to go all the way back to normal.

But as soon as she settled, a strange feeling lurked, telling her that she wasn't alone. Perhaps it was one of the guards or the servants, but it seemed peculiar considering she was usually the only one who spent time behind the palace admiring the scenery. Usually, the guards and servants would be busy at work.

Instinctively, Vira glanced back with a smile on her face. When her eyes peered down at the water again, her eyebrows drew in together. She wasn't alone, but she also hadn't recognized the man who stood near the palace walls. At least not from a distance.

Vira turned all the way around, squinting her eyes as she tried to make out who the mysterious man was. She started to walk forward. A part of her was concerned it was an intruder, and she wondered why her father hadn't given her a defense dagger.

Right, because I'm already made of fire, she thought.

The other half of her settled on the nerves and assumed it had been a peasant or mortal who was looking for something or someone, the way he stopped to peer into the window, then moved on to find some sort of entrance like he had lost something.

All Vira could make out of him was his out of place yet perfectly set ash brown hair and tall, medium build stature. His clothing seemed familiar to her, the way he had been dressed in a rather fancy white top with the collar stuck purposefully up and black pants.

"Sir, could I help you find something?" Vira called out once she had gotten close enough to him.

But the man didn't respond. He seemed rather closed off and as soon as she glanced back to see him, he immediately looked away in avoidance. Vira couldn't depict his facial expression. It seemed as if he was hiding it. But Vira knew she was the flame princess, and if the guards weren't out there to take him seriously, there was no reason she needed to wait for them to do it for her.

"Sir, can I help you find something?" she called out again, louder.

She finally approached him and mentally prepared herself to clench her fists if she needed to.

The man finally turned around all the way to face her. Vira's eyes grew wide. His complexion was like no other, immediately giving his true identity away. He was in fact, the vampire who she had struck during the war. She would remember his face anywhere.

"Yes, actually," he finally answered.

Vira caught a glimpse of his small but noticeable fangs.

She froze and said, "I'd recognize you anywhere." Her face was suddenly filled with disgust. "What are you doing here?"

"Well, I was getting to that," the vampire said passively.

"I thought I killed you," she stuttered, blinking faster than normal in shock. "You're supposed to be dead."

"Actually, when you struck me, it sent me all the way back to Wintercastle, so thank you for saving my life." His black eyes somehow sparkled as he spoke, his tone joking yet serious at the same time. "Fun fact, you have to decapitate *then* burn us in order to kill."

He leaned against the stone wall as the sun changed positions, casting a shadow in a different direction that was heading near him.

"Dad!" Vira yelled as if he would come.

Realistically, there was no way Sir Arthur, her step father, would hear her from all the way behind the castle walls. He could have been anywhere inside the palace. It had been more of an attempt to scare the vampire off.

"You can yell for your dad all you want." The vampire glared at her. "But I'm here looking for the king's crown that made my uncle the king, and I hope you remember about how there's an entire palace back at Wintercastle that is all mine by default, and you'd be able to have anything you'd like from it if you weren't so selfish." He lowered his voice and leaned into her and said, "If you'd just shut up and help me find it." His glare gave off a medusa-like effect. His stare was naturally intense enough to make her freeze with intimidation and hold her breath involuntarily.

But there were more reasons than one why no words came out of Vira's mouth at that moment. It would be a joke to say she had at least thought about it, but it would also been even more of a joke to say she wouldn't pass on helping an ice cold, blood sucking vampire who could kill her in an instant. Vira was sure they were wired to have the inability to feel empathy. They lacked a beating heart and had no soul, so how could they? And that was all the more reason that Vira scoffed at the idea.

"As much as I'd like to help you after almost killing you while you were trying to kill me, I'll have to pass." She folded her arms after unclenching her hand. "You better go back to Wintercastle right away before I kill you. Again." She raised her eyebrows. "And thank you for telling me what to do next time."

Before the vampire could even open his mouth to speak, fast footsteps came running around around the corner, revealing themself to be one of the guards, Aleski. He looked just like any other of the guards, dressed in the covering uniform. Aleski was one of the many she happened to know just by tone of voice once he spoke.

"Vira, are you alright?" He came to a halt as he approached them. "I heard you yelling for your dad."

"Yes, I..." She looked back and was shocked to find that the vampire was suddenly gone. He must have left when she'd turned. "I swear, I just saw a vampire right here," she said as she pointed where he was standing.

Aleski's eyes grew wide as he looked around. "You mean to tell me there was a vampire here?"

Vira remained in disbelief, almost wandering if she had imagined it. Perhaps she had gone insane to the point of delusion

"Y..." she stuttered. "Yes, I did, he was right here." She pointed to the wall by the window.

"They're all supposed to be dead." His voice rose in anger.

"I know, I…" She was about to explain that it was all her fault, but didn't want to give anyone more reasons to hate her than she already had. "I don't know, he must have fled or something, you know, back to Wintercastle Isle," she cryptically explained.

"Alright, well, I'm going to alert Sir Arthur immediately," he stated.

"Yes, and please let him know how I told the vampire to make his way back to where he came from, because we can easily get rid of him, too," she almost stuttered to explain.

"I'm surprised he doesn't know any better," Aleski said. He concluded their conversation when he turned to walk away and immediately headed towards the front, the closest way to get to Vira's stepfather.

Vira looked around, trying to decide whether she had just lost it or not. Perhaps there were a lot of things she had to learn about vampires. If it hadn't been for this last one, she wouldn't have had any reason to pay them any attention. She was prepared to let the war be a bygone for her own sake. But she should have known she couldn't have killed an enemy that easily during a war. She should have known she wasn't that lucky.

GUILT

O ut of the various thoughts that ran through her mind, Vira wondered what she would have gotten out of helping the vampire. As she sat at the dinner table, her stepfather seemed to pick up on her checked out state, the way she stared into the distance at the fireplace. Normally, she would never look directly at the fireplace in the dining room without the pain of seeing her mother's face. But this time, the processing of her thoughts made her blind to everything else.

Commotion gathered around the table, as many of the palace folks would join every day. They were always welcomed, but never obligated.

"Vira, baby?" her step father said.

She shook her head, shaking herself out of the trance. "Yes, hello, Father." She looked up at him and forced a smile.

"Is everything…" he looked around the table and said, "alright?"

Vira's unease was fueled by the entire table of staff looking up at her in concern. As much as she tried to hide it, her face read like a book.

She nearly choked on the water she had been sipping when she saw what felt like a hundred eyes on her. "Yes, I'm just shaken up from the war, that's all."

"Ah, well you know, we were just discussing the joy brought with how those vampires shall never be a problem again." He sounded confident.

"Ah." Vira's body temperature rose and her face felt like it turned red. "Well, of course."

Vira must have zoned out to the point she hadn't heard the conversation, or she would have known the topic was the war. Talk and commotion about the war had seemed normal, but what caught her attention was what her stepfather said about them never being a problem again.

Vira sat back in her chair and tensed up as she looked around the table, noticing Aleski had been nowhere to be seen. Perhaps he had yet to tell Vira's step father about the vampire. But that would be unusual, considering hours had passed and Aleski seemed eager to alert him right away. It hadn't been abnormal for Aleski to skip dining hours, as he had only joined once a week on a basis. But the conjunction of his absence and her step father knowing nothing about the vampire encounter struck Vira with concern.

From what Vira had heard from the commotion of the conversation, they had discussed redundant things that she had already known, such as their amends with the werewolves, and how lucky the island is to have them, or else the vampires would have made a bigger dent to the population.

But Vira's mind seemed to be the only thing she was able to listen to. It kept her company during the diner, but it had mostly been about the encounter. It was mainly due to the fact that she always felt empathy for those even if she felt she shouldn't. Her problems seemed miniscule now that she was aware about the last vampire. It had been a surprise in itself, but having the soul of everyone he knew vanish from earth seemed like an unlivable circumstance. Vira had to remind herself that they deserved it, but it also stuck with her that this man had been willing to give her something in return.

Vira looked down at the beige table cloth, pretending to admire the golden detail that held the silverware together. It was then she realized she hadn't touched the grilled chicken on her plate. So she took the silverware out of the metal holder and popped a piece into her mouth.

It dawned on her again that her step father asked why she seemed checked out, and that was a bigger deal for her. Perhaps the war did do some good for her family after all. He seemed to be in a better mood than usual, like a weight had been lifted off his shoulders. He didn't seem closed off anymore, now he was rather joyful and talkative. At that, the tables seemed to have turned. Vira had found herself to be the one who had checked out, causing her to be untalkative. But guilt was no stranger to her and this time, guilt went all around. Guilt from the hypocrisy of hoping her father would be more friendly circled her mind. But that followed also by guilt from telling off the vampire.

What hit Vira the hardest was that he had no family, nor anyone of his kind. The vampire species would die with him. All the man wanted was to look for the king's crown, so he could lead his Isle again. By now, it had probably turned into a war all in itself at Wintercastle Isle. Now she regretted her response to him. She decided maybe that she should have said yes, no matter how conflicted she was. It would have been a dirty game, but the game would have come to a clean end. He would have gone back to his Isle with what he wanted and never to be seen again, and she would have gotten what she wanted out of it. She wasn't sure what that was, but she could only imagine the possibilities. Perhaps she should have asked him what that was before yelling for her stepfather.

As a princess, she always thought she had everything she could have ever wanted. So it seemed silly to ask for more or allow anyone to bribe her. But perhaps something was still missing. Maybe not so much missing, but she had her eye on something the vampire could give her in return. Her mind circled around it. The more she thought about it, the more she couldn't quite put her finger on what that one object was.

MASKED TRUTH

The next morning, the feeling of regret and lingering guilt still hadn't worn off. Her clouded mind hadn't cleared up yet, so she settled on meditation for the morning.

The palace almost needed to install a meditation room specifically for Vira when she first gained the flame power. Her step father found it a necessary adicion since her power oftentimes wasn't controllable. Yet another thing only Vira could understand.

The only inconvenience of the meditation room was the location, which was right next to the room that housed the most dangerous reptile. Even walking past the door made Vira move feet away from it. Even then, she could still hear the sound of moist slithering and occasional hissing.

The Siciland palace was home to the Kharmat exhibit, a monstrous, venomous snake that would strip people of their powers by sucking the magic flow from their veins or worse. Every sorcerer was marked with a luminescent, glowing burn on their inner wrist that they were all given at induction. Everyone had one, including Vira. Hers was shaped as a flame.

The punishment of Kharmat's bite was only handed to those who broke rules. For some rules, they'd be sucked of their powers and their mind would be filled with amnesia and no memory of the sorcerers, as they were a secret society. Therefore, if anyone had been kicked out of the sorcerers society, they wouldn't be able to share the information with others. Others who broke the rules would have their lives taken by Kharmat. Nobody really knew what the difference would look like, not even Vira. It was rumored the reason why they were never clear about what rules had to be broken for which punishment was to keep people wondering, and to keep them from breaking any rules in fear of guessing which punishment they'd be given.

These rules included things such as sharing with others their sorcerer status, or using the power for others outside of the academy. Or any misuse, really. In the past, other sorcerers had used their power to harm one another, which would call for Kharmat's bite.

When the burn fueled Vira of her powers during the induction, it was the most pain she had ever felt in her life, aside from the news of her mother. There hadn't been much of a choice for her, though. She had to become a sorcerer if she wanted to stay a princess living in the palace. The sorcerers tended to have an odd way of dealing with things. If she had disagreed, she would have had to find a place of her own to live. And at that, she had nothing and nobody to go to. It was more so a decision between life and death. She had no predetermined gift like Altha had, where she was always a healer, even before she was given her sorcery.

The morning was still young and Vira had just approached the meditation room. After all, it wasn't often that a girl her age would just be handed an extra room all to herself simply for meditation.

When Vira opened up the door, the lighting was an orange dim with an off white glow. The smell of spearmint lingered, meant to calm her down. Subtle spa music began to play as soon as she stepped into the room and closed the door behind her.

She looked down at the palms of her hands, noticing that they heated up naturally from the heat of the room. She made her way to the mat in the center and sat. Her eyelids closed and she sat up straight. Her step father told her before to bring her attention to her fire-induced palms when she meditated to learn to control the flames inside her.

Vira's worry wasn't on her palms, though, or attempting to be mindful of them, gaining more control over what happens inside of her. It was more so about what was on her mind. Perhaps it was just from the suddenness of what happened the day prior that left her in shock and confusion. It was even strange to her that she didn't know who was in the wrong. The vampire didn't do anything to her, technically, and was simply looking for his crown. But he had the nerve to make an appearance at the palace right after his entire family was defeated.

As Vira's mind wandered, it became more and more clear to her what was right and what wasn't. She hated his guts, she really did. He was against everyone she loved, so why wouldn't she? He wouldn't want anything good for her anyhow. But he was a person too, technically. And everyone deserves decency and empathy.

It didn't matter, really. The vampire was probably long gone after Vira threatened him. He could have been back at his palace by now, or somewhere among the islands.

Perhaps Vira thought differently of him now that her mind cleared out and the anger softened. Her empathy rose for the vampire. He was all alone, and had nobody of his kind left. Everything was gone for him. What made it even worse was the fact that he had to now live eternally with the pain. To live that life would kill Vira. And here she was torn to shreds about her mother years later. Perhaps the vampire deserved something. Empathy.

Vira's eyes shot open. She couldn't believe herself for deciding that she felt bad for him and regretted not helping him. But it didn't change that fact that she did, and she knew it. It was then that she decided she was done with meditation for now. It seemed to do more harm than good and she was getting nowhere with her flame capabilities.

Vira took a deep breath before she walked out of the room and faced the palace halls. Again, she saw the guards and the servants going about their day.

Her mind was now somehow preoccupied with one person, Aleski. The guards walked the halls on one side, going opposite of her. She squinted her eyes just enough to read the name tags, then look up and offer a friendly smile. She meant to ask Aleski how everything had been for him since the vampire sighting. It hadn't been easy for Vira to know Aleski had the weight on his shoulders of being the only other person to know one of the vampires was still alive.

Once she had seen a nametag cursive with a name starting with an *A,* she smiled and waved. It had to be him. But this time, Aleski didn't reciprocate. He seemed rather nervous, like he was trying to hide something. Perhaps it was guilt, or fear. Perhaps the vampire found him and threatened to eat him had he told.

One thing Vira noticed right away was his face mask. It was unlike the guards to get sick. It covered the bottom half of his face, which left Vira wondering how he was able to breathe with everything weighing heavily on him.

It wasn't like Aleski to keep to himself. To Vira, he always seemed the friendliest of the guards, which had been the main reason Vira even knew his name in the first place, unlike many of the others.

Vira's eyebrows drew in together as she passed him. She looked back, watching Aleski walk away. He seemed to sulk, like he wasn't up for talking to anyone. But that was only by Vira's observation.

Vira continued to walk the halls in utter confusion and worry. Perhaps he was just sick and needed space, but it was stuck to Vira that the vampire had something to do with it. Either way, Vira's stomach turned at the thought of yet another, big war-initiating problem taking over the Siciland palace. Especially since they had just overcome one. It was too soon. Vira needed to know what was going on with Aleski. It was vital for her peace in mind.

THE DEAL

One thing about Vira was that she always demanded to know what she didn't.

Whatever was going on with Aleski kept Vira sitting in her room for the entirety of the afternoon in anticipation. The evening approached, and she came to terms with the fact that the questions circling in her mind weren't going to leave. She didn't fancy the idea of spending the night awake, letting her mind run with all the possibilities as she attempted to calm her own pulse down. She would always close her eyes and attempt to fall asleep, but that never brought the thoughts to an ease. It seemed to only allow them more room to speak.

So Vira knew what she wanted to do next. She had to find Aleski.

When Vira made her way out into the hallway, the guards weren't anywhere within eye shot, but she knew they had to be within the premises. The guards were oftentimes quiet and Aleski would be difficult to find amongst the group of them who usually walked together, but surely it wouldn't be impossible to track him down.

Vira walked the halls back toward where the guards slept. They would normally take turns on and off, but Aleski surely wouldn't be asleep just yet.

A group of guards approached her. They were quiet for the most part. They never chatted amongst each other to keep the professionalism. But Vira at least needed to have an idea of where Aleski was in order to track him to the point where she would be able to talk to him all alone.

Vira passed the group of lined up guards. Even the way they walked was in tune, none of them missing a beat. But last time Vira saw Aleski, he wasn't walking like the others, which was what threw her off, drawing her eyes to him first.

Vira's eyes squinted as she attempted to read the name tag of the guards who had passed her, but they had come and gone too fast.

Her pulse raced as she started to panic over trying to find him. At this point, she had been creeping around the palace to find this man. Soon, people would know she was starting to act strange and Vira was not a good liar. Suddenly the guards seemed to notice her interest in them and it immediately put Vira on edge. The three guards turned around and called her name.

It was a foolish feeling for Vira to realize Aleski had a face mask on, and that looking at nametags would have been the hard way to find him.

One of them asked with no suspicion, "Madam, may I help you with something?"

"Oh, I…" She looked around in panic. "No, I just…" No words came out of her mouth. There was a moment of silence in the hallway. An awkward one.

The guards collectively cocked their heads at her, confused. "Alrighty then," one of them said as they turned around and continued their walk around.

Vira turned back around as her heart persisted to pound. She caught a glimpse of a guard walking in the distance in the hallway. He seemed to have a face mask on. Vira's eyes widened. He was all alone with nobody in sight, which was even better. But it was unlike Aleski to go out of his way to walk alone, which seemed strange. Perhaps the vampire sighting really got to him.

Vira kicked off her heels and picked them up. She paced down the hallway after him, keeping her gaze in his direction. She thought about calling his name, but it would echo, and at the moment, she wanted to maintain a low profile. Although, having a panic attack when the guards asked her if she was looking for someone probably hadn't helped either. In fact, it was as she had gotten close enough to him and stopped to put her heels back on that she realized she could have made something up on the spot, like she had been searching for her step father, or the woman who tailored her dress.

Aleski glanced back at Vira only half way, but just enough so she couldn't quite see his eyes.

"Aleski?" she called out once she was within a few feet of him and she could talk quietly enough to the point it wouldn't echo.

Still, there was still no answer. Just a sulky stature as he walked.

But Vira continued to follow him, concerned. By now she had known something had to have been up with him, and whatever it was, it was no good. She knew Aleski, and he was all for helping her when she needed it. There was no way he would shut her out of a situation only the two of them knew about.

It had seemed that he was leading her somewhere when he turned left out to the back entrance, a turn guards would normally never go near.

"Uh, Aleski, should I be concerned?" she asked as she continued to follow him.

But still, no answers came from him. He straightened his posture as he approached the door, then opened it without looking back or holding it open for Vira behind him.

Vira's eyebrows drew together. She wondered if he knew how disrespectful he was acting, especially to the princess. To not hold the door for the princess was not just frowned upon, but nearly forbidden. Even that would be an understatement. In fact, he probably hoped the other guards wouldn't find out.

She now followed close behind him outside. His anxiousness started to show in the way he half glanced back yet again, then quickly looked straight ahead. Something about her wanting to talk to him made him uneasy, and she couldn't understand why. Perhaps the vampire he had an encounter with told him not to tell anyone, and Vira was a part of that deal. But that had been the only excuse Vira could ponder at the moment.

The clock struck down time, which was eight in the evening, and the bells played loudly. Aleski was surprisingly startled by it, causing him to jerk in startle and fall on the ground. Vira had gotten used to the loud bells, as she knew they were always coming, but she thought Aleski would know better.

Aleski fell on his back causing his hat to topple off.

"Aleski, are you okay?" Vira asked, concerned. The situation freaked her out a lot, and something about it clearly wasn't right. But she had him backed into a corner now, so she knew she was about to find out what caused his strange behavior.

As soon as it fell off his head, his eyes grew wide, and so did Vira's.

Only it wasn't Aleski's eyes, but the vampire's black eyes surrounded by his grayish pale skin that seemed to be triggered by the sunlight exposure hitting his skin.

Vira gasped. She watched him panic as he struggled to put the guard hat back on. She couldn't believe it. She knew she regretted their first encounter, but her first reaction was wondering where Aleski was. Her stomach turned sour and bile splashed to the top of her throat.

The vampire ran into the forest that, out of the two of them, only Vira knew turned into a secluded open garden area shaded by thick trees. Part of her panic stemmed from knowing she made a life threatening move by following him into the secluded area. Perhaps he'd eat her just as he did Aleski. Yet, curiosity got the best of her and she demanded to know what was going on

"Stop!" she yelled.

Her heart dropped when he did, and he turned around slowly with a grim look on his face.

She gulped in fear as she said, "Thank you."

He stared at her in silence. The way he flared his eyes made him look hungry, perhaps an attempt to scare her off.

"Wh…" she stuttered, feeling that if she spoke, vomit would come out too. She choked down the bile before saying. "Who are you, what did you do to Aleski?"

The vampire took off both the hat and mask before saying anything. His eyebrows drew together and his eyes looked her up and down like he clearly had something against her. "Nothing."

Vira folded her arms. She didn't even need to tell him she knew that wasn't true.

"Meaning, I didn't kill him." He shook his head. His voice was deep and mysterious, leaving Vira apprehensive to ask more questions.

But Vira's pulse slowed down when she heard him confess that there was apparently nothing *to* confess.

"What did you do with him?" she demanded.

"He's…" The vampire looked around like he was gathering his thoughts. "He's somewhere, in a survivable condition, but I can't give him back his uniform until I," he paused, then quietly chuckled. "Well, you know what I want," he said, petting the rim of the guard hat.

"I do," she nodded. "But where is he?"

"He's secluded in a cabin bolted shut with water and rice. Don't worry. I won't kill him. Just so long as I get what I want." His face went grim again.

"Why would you do this?" Vira's forehead crinkled as she asked.

The vampire looked at her like she had an extra head.

"I mean, why didn't you just kill him?" she clarified.

"Well," he looked down with a slight grin and said, "I didn't want to be *that* cruel."

Vira went silent. A vampire not wanting to be cruel? It made no sense at all. They were stone cold killers, weren't they?

"So," she looked him up and down with a look of disapproval like he had done to her, "the king's crown?" she asked cryptically.

He went into shock when she eased up on him. "Well, yes," he nodded. "It was my uncle's, who was the king. By default, I'm now the king of Wintercastle Isle. And I need it to do my job," he explained.

"And you can't get a new one?" she asked.

The vampire shook his head. "It's been in the family for centuries."

"I'm a princess and my stepfather is the ruler of Siciland," she said. "We just went to war with you."

The vampire looked at her yet again like there was something wrong with her. "Yes," he nodded slowly. "And I understand, but you know I have a palace all to myself now. Whatever you want, I'll supply it if you just help me find the crown," he said. He was clearly too petty and arrogant to plead for it.

Vira just stood there. She knew she changed her mind when it came to their first interaction, and the guilt and empathy she had for him was real, but it was tough to have to make that decision again now that she was faced with him once more, staring at him as the moonlight gradually made its appearance.

But the vampire's facial expression shifted from grim to doubtful.

He broke both the silence. "And if I end up dead, don't cry, don't be scared, don't even empathize with me," he said emotionless.

Vira thought for a moment that everything was true and it would be a dire mistake. Maybe she was helping someone with not just a heart that doesn't beat, but someone who can't feel love at all.

"Why?" she asked.

"Because," he shook his head in doubt, "if I have to live a life where everyone I love is dead and I'm alone in the world, then that," he paused, squeezing his eyes shut in pain, "is a world not worth living in."

Vira wanted to cry. Now, she didn't know what to believe in. She thought of her own situation, and everyone she had ever loved had gone away with the exclusion of her stepfather who, really, she wasn't sure about most of the time. He never tucked her in when she was a little girl or sang her lullabies. He never even kissed the cuts on her knees when she fell down, or even did the bare minimum, by offering to grab her a bandage.

Perhaps he was trying to convince her to pity him. That, too, was a possibility.

Before Vira could say a word, the vampire kept going, "You know what?" he took a deep breath and said, "go ahead," like it had pained him to say.

Vira raised an eyebrow in confusion as she said, "Go ahead and what?"

The vampire kneeled down to one knee and said, "Do the honors, decapitate me."

Perhaps he wasn't trying to get her pity if he was willing to go as far to let her kill him while she had the chance.

50

"What?" Her voice went high pitched.

"Really, all that I just said made me realize that I don't even want to be here anymore. I shouldn't be here, in fact." He bobbed his head toward her and said, "Do it. You wish me dead anyway."

Vira thought of her step father as she stepped closer to him, and with that, also came the thought of all the other citizens of Siciland. She would be, in secret, doing them all a huge favor. It would reset everything for her and she'd be able to live the life she lived before she had made the mistake of meeting the vampire. And at that, he'd never bother anyone ever again.

Vira stepped behind him and placed her gloved hands onto his neck. She moved one of them up to his chin, pulling it towards herself. Suddenly, a cold chill flew down her spine, not just from the cold touch of his ice cold skin even through the thin gloves. She hadn't even really known why her sudden unease felt like she was doing the one thing everyone else wanted. It felt unfair that she was the one who was faced with this decision.

Vira strengthened her grip as she started to turn the head back towards herself. She could hear tiny cracks in his jaw. In the midst of decapitating him, she stopped. She felt like she couldn't go through with it. She threw herself back in a jerk, her heart pounding heavily feeling like it took up her entire chest.

He looked back at her suddenly mortified facial expression. "Aren't you going to finish the job?" he asked.

"I…" She took a deep breath. She stepped back from him and she rubbed her hands together vigorously to warm them back up. She couldn't. She just couldn't. And she should have known. Something urged her to hate him, but something urged her even more to help him for her own sake somehow.

The vampire's face lit up with a look of hope as he pushed himself up and stood firmly with his hands interlaced at his abdomen.

"Dracula, you need to promise me one thing." She backed up as she cleared her throat, shaking the worry out of herself.

"Cassius," he corrected her.

"Huh?" Vira cocked her head.

"Cassius. My name is Cassius and my surname is Strike," he explained, clearly irritated by her deliberate mis-speak. "And what is it that I have to promise you?"

Vira shook her head like she was irritated as well, but by his correction. "That you'll go back to your Isle, and never come here again. You're dead for all everyone else knows."

"Yes, I know," he nodded. "According to everyone else I'm soulless and emotionless. Oh yeah, and a stone cold killer."

"You're what now?" she asked.

"Yeah, I've heard the conversations that go on around the palace even within my first couple of hours," he explained.

Vira's heart felt heavy for only a second when she realized his life for what it was. He was the last vampire alive, and all of his family members were dead. He, indeed, had nobody. But he sure didn't have anything. At that point, at least helping him until he found his crown felt like the only morally right thing to do. But she still couldn't tell if Cassuis was being sarcastic or not. What he said seconds ago about his love for his family made her think differently, but his words about being a murderer seemed to differ with each sentence. She was still conflicted towards him, but now she knew she demanded to know another thing. She demanded to know if he had emotions or not.

"So," Cassius broke a pitiful moment of silence. "Let me know what it is that you *actually* want in return."

"I sure will." Vira nodded. "Just as long as you go back to your isle after the quest is over and never come back."

"I sure will," he mocked her. "You'll never see my face again."

"Great. I can't wait," she said surely.

"I just have one question," he said. "Is there anything we can do about the guard once we release him?"

Vira had forgotten all about Aleski. She tapped her chin as her mind wandered through ideas. But then, she remembered. "There's a snake."

"A snake?" he asked.

"Yes, his name is Kharmat. We usually only use him on us sorcerers to punish people, but he sucks the memory out of people who have been kicked out of the sorceres' secret society so they don't remember anything and can't tell. We'd be able to replace you with him once you're done here," she explained.

"Ah, so it does work out now," he nodded.

"You know, for a vampire who is, like, three hundred and something years old," Vira joked, "you don't seem to think things through."

"Some things never change." He shook his head. "Some joke that I haven't matured past one hundred and nine."

Perhaps he was just desperate and careless for the king's crown and hadn't thought his plan through in a panic.

"I suppose you're not so bright either, Miss accidentally-shoots-me-all-the-way-back-to-Wintercastle-Isle," he joked.

"I wasn't prepared. We didn't know you were vampires, and for the record, I knew nothing about you guys or how to kill you," she explained.

"And I just gave you permission for a do-over, and you still didn't take your chance," he one-upped her.

"Well don't worry. I think I know what to do now if this ever gets out of hand." She folded her arms. "And as long as we're comparing carelessness, you didn't need to tell me how to kill you. That was on you."

"Ah." He tried to hide his small grin. "I think we're even then."

Vira looked up, noticing the sky had gone completely dark at that point.

"You're right." Vira nodded. "We better get back to the palace before anyone comes looking for either of us, Aleski."

Cassius nodded. "But what will happen next?"

"I live in the room with the biggest door at the end of the hallway near the stairs. You'll know it when you see it. Make sure nobody is around when you slide paper notes under my door. We need to avoid being seen with each other as much as possible to avoid suspicion. The only thing I'd ever been caught doing with Aleski is waving at him."

"Okay." He lowered his voice to a loud whisper. "Sounds like a plan."

Vira nodded, then turned around to make her way out of the secluded garden while glancing back at him every other second as she made her way to the door. It was a good thing that he hadn't followed close behind her, because it was fully nighttime and they would know her and Aleski had some sort of secretiveness going on. And at Siciland Palace, secretiveness of any type was pried into and strictly forbidden.

STEP ONE

T he first person who came to Vira's mind as soon as the morning sun hit was Altha.

The battleground location was between Altha's area and her werewolf mate Zereck's. She had to have known at least something about where the lost crown could be. One thing Vira knew was it had to have fallen off the head of the king shortly before or merely after his death. Perhaps it was still on the battlefield. But it would be of no mind to have the vampire search to find it, as he would be decapitated right on the scene and his body would be thrown into the ocean by the wolves who resided a short distance from the scene. So this morning, Vira knew what her plan was as she was making her bed.

Altha was supposed to arrive in the morning as well. Perhaps she'd be at the palace soon. Vira knew the obstacle she'd cross when talking to Altha. It was by convenience that Altha was the closest one to Vira at the palace, but still, telling her about Cassius would be game over. And it wasn't worth risking that early on.

A small folded piece of paper caught Vira's attention when she glanced around her room. The morning would have been filled with meditation to help with her out of control powers like the day before, but it had seemed to slip her mind the second she grabbed the paper from the floor near the door. She knew right away it had to be from Cassius.

Remembering what had happened the night before hit Vira's mind like a tidal wave of doubt and anxiety. She worried immensely about what would happen if she had gotten caught helping him and just the fact of knowing he had gotten away with roaming around Siciland Palace by no agreement but her own.

Vira unfolded the paper all the way until she could read it. His handwriting looked to be a mix between cursive and not. She started interpreting it.

Vira,

I have gotten a chance to pace around the palace. I've been attempting to keep a low profile and thus far, I am lucky to have nobody approach me. I'll be pacing near the back entrance if you need me. I haven't found anything worth snooping yet, but I am sure you'd know if I did.

-Cassius

Cassius seemed to hang out near the back door of the palace a lot, similarly to when she had followed him outside. She expected it to be his normal go to hiding place from now on. It was probably in both of their favor to do so with the small number of other guards who rarely show themselves near the back. That would be the best place for them to talk anyways as it was a more secluded area and without anyone around to see through their suspicious behavior.

But Vira still wanted to wait for Altha before speaking to him. She would better know the situation and be able to give him more information. She still wanted to spend her time with him sparingly for a couple of reasons. He only fueled her guilt and every time she thought of him she hated herself more. At least when he wasn't around she could forget about him to a degree. If he did happen to get caught, she'd play dumb and go along with everyone else who would immensely despise even knowing of his existence.

By then it was already near early afternoon, so Vira made an effort to leave her bedroom and hope Altha had nobody in her office.

As she walked the halls, Cassius was nowhere to be seen, which was actually a good thing.

Vira passed by Altha's office and casually stopped. She walked backwards as she peered into the doorway to catch Altha talking on the phone. She seemed to have been talking to Zereck, or someone who made her light up when talking to.

She noticed Vira standing in the doorway and immediately asked the person she was talking to if she was able to call them back, and that she had just started her work day.

Once she set the phone back on the wall, she stood up to Vira with an immediate smile.

"Sorry, I didn't mean to interrupt," Vira said as she stood in the doorway.

"No, no, it's okay." She shook her head in assurance. "That was Zereck. We're going to rebuild our house very soon, we just got the news." She almost squealed in excitement.

Vira smiled as well. "That's great, you deserve it."

For as long as Altha's life was flipped upside down, she lived in a one room dome of a house. She was in deep poverty, but ever since she became the healer at the palace, she had been heading up the path of wealth. Everything seemed to turn up for her, even if she had to go through, literally, war and back to get it.

"I know, nothing excites me more right now than finally building a livable space," she boasted.

"Yeah, I bet." Vira didn't mean to come off underwhelmed for her, but preoccupation and worry of finding the crown was what crowded her brain and robbed her mind of better thoughts.

"Are you okay?" Altha's excitement faded into concern.

"Oh yes." Vira stepped farther into the room and cleared her throat. "Listen," she shut the door behind her, "I lost an earring during the battle and it's valuable to me. Do you know where any of the valuables were taken after cleaning the battleground?"

Altha paused in anticipation. After thinking, she finally said, "I think I'd have to ask Zereck."

Vira wasn't thrilled to hear that, but at least she knew she would get somewhere by asking.

"Oh." She made herself smile anyways. "That would be great."

"I'll ask him tonight once I get home. I'll let you know what I hear tomorrow," Altha explained.

Out of all people, Vira was grateful only Altha would know about the remnants of the vampire's belongings.

"So, where are the vampires now?" Vira asked.

"Dead."

"But, I mean, when you were all cleaning up the battleground, what did you do with them?" Vira specified.

"The shifter wolves tossed them in the ocean," Altha explained.

That wasn't good news for Vira's sake. The king surely tumbled to the ground once he was taken down, meaning hopefully his crown rolled back somewhere. And hopefully, just hopefully, they only threw the vampires themselves into the ocean.

"Ah, I see." Vira nodded. "Do you know what they may have done with any of the valuables after the war that were left behind?"

"Well," she exhaled and thought. "The wolves don't care much for shiny objects, so the chance that they did something careless with them, like rip them to shreds and then laugh about it."

Vira nodded her head, but felt doubtful on the inside.

"But there's also the chance that they're at the palace; your step father probably requested them to be sent here."

Now that Vira thought about it, she had no idea which option was more believable.

"Your earring," Altha said.

Vira looked up to see the sideways look Altha had.

"What did it look like?" she asked.

"Well, it was…" Vira's anxiety came when Altha questioned her. She had to think fast. She had to say anything. "It was golden, and it was long." She tried to be cryptic. "At least, I think I lost it at the war."

"Ah." Altha nodded.

But Vira still felt the need to justify herself. "I normally have them on, but when I came home from the war, it was nowhere to be seen."

"I'll keep that in mind when I talk to Zereck," Altha said.

Perhaps Vira realized then that she shouldn't have asked Altha what they did with the dead vampires, but it was worth the knowledge.

"Thanks, Al." She nodded awkwardly before turning around and walking out.

Vira's paranoid self believed now that Altha picked up on her mannerisms. It would be a while, if at all, that Vira even thought about coming clean to Altha. It would really show where their friendship stood. But finding out wasn't worth the risks as fresh as the situation was.

She wondered if the clicking of her heels was too loud as she made her way to the back of the castle to approach Cassius. It would be smarter to stay as quiet as she could to avoid anyone hearing that she was headed that way.

Vira took a turn inside her room and threw her heels just inside the door. It was by luck that she was wearing a longer gown this morning, so nobody would be able to tell her footwear of choice.

Vira made her way down the hallway like she normally would and peered inside the guard's bunk room to see if Cassius was in there. Luckily, she could tell by the time she walked past that there was no sign of him. That was a good thing because the more Cassius was near the guards, the easier it would be for them to be onto him. The main indicator of him was the facemask he had on. Soon enough, he'd be asked about it. It dawned on Vira that the mask would be an issue in terms of flying under the radar.

She soon caught a glimpse of him standing stiff near the back door. She looked around several times before approaching him. Luckily, nobody was near yet. She planned on making the conversation quick to avoid the fear of someone catching on to their suspicious behavior.

"Cassius," she whispered. "I've got some news."

"Let's hear it," he whispered back.

"Altha will know what happened to the crown after the war. She'll give us news tomorrow," Vira said.

Cassuis nodded, somewhat underwhelmed just like Vira had been when she heard they had to wait to know if the crown was even among the four walls of the palace. He seemed to want the crown now, not later. At least, he didn't seem excited to wait days on end before getting it, drawing out the painful thrill of a process.

"Has anyone approached you about it, you know?" Vira motioned to her mouth where the mask was on Cassius.

He shook his head and whispered, "No, but I can feel eyes on me already."

Vira's eyebrows raised. "That's what I was afraid of. Somehow let them know your voice is gone and you can't talk."

"Actually," she second guessed herself. Vira realized Altha had the power to cure that within seconds, so it wouldn't make any sense. "Keep it on until further notice."

Cassuis cocked an eyebrow. "Do you really think it could be an issue?" he asked.

"I just don't want anyone approaching you and asking about it. It might blow the cover," Vira explained.

She grew stressed at the fact that their plan was clearly flawed. Surely she'd think of some way to cover up the fact that Aleski was covering his face for a reason other than he was replaced by a forbidden vampire.

"See, I thought this would take a day. Maybe two," he argued.

"Well," Vira exhaled in stress. "I don't know. I'm sure it still can."

"I didn't want to spend any more time here than I needed," he complained.

"I'll hear back from Altha tomorrow. I'll let you know, but for now, slip me notes when the halls are vacant," she suggested.

"Alright." Cassius squeezed his eyelids tight and rubbed his forehead. "Yet, you still need to figure out what you'd like in return," he opened his eyes and said.

"Ah," she looked up in anticipation. "I forgot all about that."

"Well, you better decide quickly," he nodded.

"Yes, I will, I'll come up with an answer for you tonight," she concluded when her eyes grew wide as footsteps approached from afar.

Before he could even answer, Vira took off into a different direction. She made her way back to the center of the palace to head back to her room.

One thing that left a bad taste in Vira's mouth was Cassius's arrogance. All she had done was help him, yet he still had the same petty, arrogant attitude from when they first spoke. Perhaps vampires didn't have a heart, or manners. A small feeling of regret trickled into her mind, but one small bit of hope still kept her company. Him asking what she would want in return. The possibilities were limitless and being unable to decide was more of a good problem to have.

MAD THIRST

One of the only things Vira felt an emotional connection to was the creation of art. From the moment she got to her room after another mentally checked out dinner with her step father and other people of the palace, she felt the urge to relax and paint for the rest of the night.

The entire dinner went similar to the day prior. Thankfully, the one thing different was no attention came her way. Not that she wasn't used to being ignored, but it had come to her benefit this time around.

Vira's thoughts gathered themselves as she sat on the leather chair of her vanity in front of a blank canvas and the paint palette sat on a side table next to her. Luckily, she wore nothing but her robe and undergarments, as it would be a big problem for her had her gown attained even had speck of paint. Not because she was overly worried, but it was unwashable, and her step father would be enraged with her for needing to spend more on a gown she had tens of variations of.

She dreamed that it would be nice to have a gallery of paintings, but she would only paint in secret. She suspected that she would be judged for it, even if she didn't know why. Other than that, the main reason it felt like her hobby of painting should be kept a secret was because no one ever asked what she loved to do other than wear dresses, which isn't really a hobby.

Finally, she picked up the paintbrush and swirled it in sky blue paint, then painted it thin on the canvas around the edges to start a background. She wove the strokes together, creating an ice blue image of the beginning of a sky.

From time to time, she'd look up from the painting to glance around her room. She played a game with herself, thinking of things she doesn't have that she'd want to try and decide on something Cassius could reward her with.

Jewelry not only wasn't her thing, but she already had too much of it. It would also be useless for her interest to add onto the collection she already had. The next thing she knew the answer wouldn't be was a crown of her own. Not only did she already have one, but she'd be in question of where she had gotten it. It would be nice to have company, maybe a bird like her father had in his office. But it wasn't for sure that the vampire's palace would have very many animals. Or maybe they did. Or maybe, Vira realized she was just pulling things out of nowhere. Her step father couldn't stand Flaps, his fat, black, obnoxious bird. He was beyond obnoxious. It seemed to her like she was kidding herself at that point.

Vira stared at one of her dresses as she painted lines that mimicked the shape of it with a sunny orange color. The more she gazed in the direction of her dress, the more she painted what looked similar to it without even noticing. That led her mind to ponder another thing, she wouldn't need a dress or clothes either. She already had too much of it. But needless to say, she knew she'd figure it out. There had to be something she didn't have yet. She wondered how she was even supposed to know what Cassius had in his palace. Perhaps she should have asked him that. The vampires run differently. They have a different culture than the sorcerers in Siciland.

Just as Cassius came to her mind, Vira heard the sound of paper sliding in from under her door. She looked over in the direction and saw the piece of paper sitting in front of it. It was obviously from Cassius. An unexpected thrill of excitement hit her. Perhaps it was just a sense of relief of knowing that he hadn't been caught yet and their cover hadn't been blown.

Vira walked over and picked up the paper, reading it after straightening out the crinkles with her thumb.

Vira,

I have yet to hear anything about the vampires other than how much we are hated. No word on anything from anyone. After you hear back from your friend, we have to do some digging tomorrow at minimum. No exceptions. If it's here, you ought to know where it could be. If it's somewhere else, then I'll head there. I'm growing sick of hearing my kind mentioned in vain, and before I can stop myself, I'll suck someone dry.

-Cassius

Vira's eyes grew wide. Perhaps, the content of the note was too strong for her. She opened up her vanity and set the note on top of the other one where she stacked them. She understood why Cassius was growing tired, but it was weighing on her too. It would've been wiser to burn the notes before someone else found them, but something inside her told her to keep them, so she did.

She left the, so far, painted canvas where it was, but took the paint palette to the sink in her bathroom to wash it off. That would be enough painting for the day. She thought she was getting somewhere, gathering her thoughts and ignoring the angst that came with sneaking a vampire into the palace, but now there was a whole new set of problems. She knew she needed to find the crown and she needed it fast. That was the only way this would end well for anyone.

Clearly, a new day would bring hope that it would at least start to work out, but the only way to get to that fast was by a good nights' rest.

Vira stuck the paint palette back to the side of the canvas. Then she realized it was out in the open. She hated that no privacy was allowed in the palace. So she moved the easel behind her vanity, so nobody would see it at first glance if they walked in the room. But then she asked herself why she felt the need to hide her innocent hobby of painting. And at that, she had no answer either.

THE MAP

The morning started early for Vira. Nervous jitters caught up to her and the feeling of eagerness ran excitement throughout her entire body.

The heels of Vira's shoes clicked down the halls as fast as she paced to Altha's office. She took no time to wait around. As soon as she was due to be at the office, she knew what she had to do. Perhaps the crown being on the battlefield would be a good thing, leading Cassius to leave the palace to be someone else's problem. But then Aleski would still be Vira's issue. He was still stranded wherever Cassius took him.

When Vira approached Altha's office, she knocked on the doorframe to get her attention.

"Altha, hi." She came across as friendly so she could get information faster.

"Vira, hi," she mimicked.

"So…" She wanted to get straight to the point, but at the same time show gratitude that her friend was helping her. "Have you heard anything?"

Altha nodded, "Any of the valuable things that were left on the battleground were on the Maycaster side, which is under your stepfather's rule."

"So, what does that mean?" Vira asked.

"Zereck, or anyone in Davelburn, would have no chance of having it. It was all taken back to the palace and kept."

In some ways, Vira wished Zereck did have it. It would mean Cassius would be on his way and find it there. But at the same time, she knew it wouldn't pan out the way she wanted either way. Cassius would get caught, then eaten. That wouldn't help anything in the situation.

In that case, Vira was sure she'd be brought down with him if anything and they'd both be in danger.

So the news was rather good. At least her actions hadn't been for nothing.

"Thanks," she nodded with a smile. "I'll go ask my father then," she responded.

"Ah," Altha nodded. "If you don't mind me asking, why didn't you ask Sir Arthur in the first place?"

Vira's pulse rose. "I…" She thought about it, trying to come up with a reasonable enough answer. "That's a good question," she nervously laughed. "Why didn't I think of that?" was all she could think to say.

"Yeah," Altha matched the nervous laugh. "I know."

Vira shook her head. It wasn't like her to be so careless, but when nerves got to her, she'd let accidents slip. Although, realistically, her and her step father didn't have constant dialogue in the first place. After all, what she did say was nothing out of the norm. If only Altha had known how distant their relationship was.

"Alright then, well, I better get to work," Altha concluded.

"Oh, right." Vira shook her head again. "I'm sorry to keep you waiting," she concluded, turning away and stepping out of the office.

Now, she knew she needed to find Cassius and let his short fused self know they had to start looking right away. He was the one who needed the crown, and now they were able to find it and not feel aimless about their search. It was beneficial they asked Altha first, not that they knew exactly where it was but more so, that, now, they were at least sure the crown was within the palace's walls.

Vira headed towards the back of the palace where Cassius had been previously. It was a bit surprising that she hadn't woken up to another note this morning, but perhaps it was a good thing, as there had probably been nothing to tell.

The faint figure of Cassius became more clear in the distance. He seemed to be pacing around the back door as she made her way there. He must not have known much about guards, or how to be a guard, anyways.

But she caught his eye, and he stopped pacing. He walked behind an indent in the wall once he knew she saw him. It was hard to tell if he was angry or not. His expression still hadn't become clear once Vira slid behind the indent of the wall as well, where no view of him nor her would be able to be seen by anyone walking by.

She looked straight into his jett black eyes as soon as she was in front of him.

He lifted down his mask, revealing the paler color of his skin.

"So?" he asked, eager.

"It's here." She pointed to the ground.

"What do you mean, here?" he asked.

"It's somewhere in the palace," she specified.

"We have to do some digging, then." He seemed nothing but eager. Perhaps the note from the previous night had been out of anger, which meant good news that Vira didn't have to worry about Cassius losing control and biting someone's head off.

"Like you said." She motioned to him.

"You know this place better than me." He leaned on the wall and said, "Where do we start?"

Vira rolled her eyes towards the back of her. "You'd be surprised," she said.

"You're the princess, Vira. I feel like you'd have to know." His eyebrows drew in together.

"I don't really get called *the princess* a lot," she corrected him. "And trust me, my step father and I never talk."

"You don't?" He was taken aback. His gaze deepened in sorrow.

"No, but I'll be able to make my way to anywhere in the palace," she explained.

The palace was huge. Vira had gotten lost in it too many times to count. But by now, there was no reason she wouldn't be able to find something specific. After all, she was looking for a valuable item said to be an earring. She'd be able to use that if she was ever in question.

"I'd…" Cassius leaned in and lowered his voice. "Appreciate it if you could scope out a few places to start."

Vira nodded her head in agreement. For sure, his lowering of voice wasn't to keep a secret anymore. The softness in his voice was to keep her going, hoping that she'd want to help him more by subtly and innocently enticing her. But she could see right through his fluorescent motives. And talking low was *not* enough to entice her, even if it worked a little bit.

"I know we have maps around here." Vira bit her bottom lip. "I'd guess they're in the library if they were anywhere."

"And that would give us an idea of where to look?" He finally got excited about something.

"Yes, but I'd like you to look around too," she ordered. "You never know what we could find."

"Got it, split up." He nodded his head.

First, Vira walked out from the hiding place in the wall. She ran around the corner fast so nobody knew where she had come from.

The library wasn't far from where she was. In fact, it was just past the dining hall. Vira looked back and watched Cassius resume his pace of the palace like the other guards would.

The dining hall hadn't even been set for lunch yet, but Vira never cared for the lunch part of the day anyway. She would normally spend it outside by the stream or the courtyard flower garden. She caught the aroma of the soups and sandwiches of the buffet cooking, though. Usually everything in the palace that was made by the kitchen staff smelled fiercely of garlic.

But once Vira had gotten past that and opened the big, glass doors leading to the library, the room of wonder stood before her. The big, ancient looking books caught her eye and were on her mind from the beginning. She knew that all the books of the palace that were more important were the ones that were older.

So she made her way to the shelf where they stood. She looked around, admiring the shelves of hundreds, if not, thousands of books, and the fact that she had the library all to herself. Nobody was around to question her actions, which eased her worries.

Vira moved her ball gown so she could hunch down after she picked up the biggest book. It was titled, *Siciland Palace,* and should be the only book that would have a map of the palace in it.

She opened it up and flipped past old pages chock full of words she didn't need to read. The middle struck her when she noticed the gold foil lining on just those pages. When she turned to them, the two pages spread apart into the palace from an above perspective, showing the insides of the castle. Her eyes went right to where her room was, which she would base all the locations off of and how to get to each one.

The shadow of a servant walking by frightened Vira as it came from the side of the hallway. It was the panic that made her rip the two pages right out of the book and stuff them in her thankfully roomy dress pockets. Almost immediately, she stood up from crouching down and set the book back on the shelf where it was before and rushed back to her room.

＊

Vira's eyes traced over every turn of the maze of a palace on the map. For as long as she had lived at the palace, there were more rooms she'd never been in than not. For the most part, she'd find herself pondering near the garden, or by the stream if she wasn't in her room or joined by her father during dinner hour.

There were only a handful of places, though, this valuable crown could possibly have been. She took a thick red inked pen and circled the only three that stuck out to her.

The first one that she for sure knew would be possible was the old room of her mother. She always had the most valuable items in her possession in terms of jewelry. The amount of gems and diamonds were more than she'd need even in several lifetimes, but regardless, if Vira's step father ever found jewelry or any precious diamonds on something, sometimes he'd set it in her room as if he was giving it to her.

But Vira hadn't gone to her mothers room in ages. It was always too hard for her. Thinking of the old memories like when her mother would allow her to bounce on her bed or read her a story, or sing to her when she felt down, would hit Vira like bricks.

The next place on the map she circled was the valuable museum storage room. The valuables included items that would be displayed in the exhibit part of the palace. There looked to be an exact location for the tiny room where they'd store the artifacts. The history of the war, now that it had become history, was one of the greatest defeats of all time in Siciland. There'd be no reason to withhold the vampire king's crown as part of that. And even more, there would be no way they wouldn't display the recognition the island got for the great defeat of the vampires.

One last location struck Vira: her step father's vault. Apparently he would keep valuable items in a safe. But Vira didn't know that. She never knew he had a safe at all. It suddenly hit her that a king's crown was more than valuable. It could be worth trillions if they were still alive. However, Cassius needed the crown more than Vira's stepfather, and she knew that. Vira also knew her step father. He'd be a snob all day long. In every lifetime. But that was all the more reason to remind herself that she wouldn't be taking anything away from him, but giving it to someone who needed and valued it.

Yet another piece of paper slid from under her door. It was perfect timing, as she had just finished scoping out the entire map for any and all possible places where the crown could be.

She picked up the note and unrolled it. She seemed to only be seeing Cassius once a day, so these notes worked out for the better to keep herself out of the mess.

Vira,

Splitting up was a bad idea. Not only was I approached, but I was approached by whom I believe was your dearest friend Altha. She asked me if I needed a dose of Coughing Lily, whatever that means, and I respectfully declined. She gave me a strange look afterward, which made me shriek. We may have to switch up our tactics and try something new. I hope you're not tired, because I'd like you to meet me by the secluded area in the forest where we have previously encountered each other if you don't believe you'd be caught there. We have a lot to discuss as it seems. The night time is better for me anyways, when most of the other guards are asleep and I'm not. They'd best believe I'm double shifting.

-Cassius

It had gotten even worse than anticipated. The plan seemed to be going downhill by the hour. At least it was down to three places in the entire palace to search. The pressing urge to find the crown progressively worsened.

Vira peered out her window, noticing that the sky was past the deep blue shade of the evening and the moon was already glowing up in the sky. It was shocking for her to realize that she had mapped her entire afternoon away, so she thought she'd grab something to eat before meeting up with Cassius. She shoved the marked map in the pocket of her dress and took off.

THE QUEENS' ROOM

As Vira made her way down the hall to the kitchen, barely anyone stayed out to roam the halls, which was a good thing. Even just the sight of people made Vira uneasy now.

It was a challenge to tiptoe softly down the halls barefoot again to avoid any noise she didn't want others to hear. She chose a turkey sandwich to eat to avoid crunching noises, as any of the other food options would cause.

Just before Vira stepped out of the back palace door, she swallowed the last bit of the sandwich. She wondered how long Cassius had been waiting for her out in the unpleasantly chilled breeze. Not that the temperature was supposed to bother him.

It was a struggle for Vira to make her way through as she pushed her way through the branches of the trees as the wind blew her hair in front of her face several times. The chilly temperature didn't bother her though as her natural unusually high body temperature warmed her up instantly.

She pushed the last branch out of the way, revealing Cassius sitting on the bench with the guard hat sitting beside him.

"Cassius?" she called out, nearly being choked by the wind.

He stood up and took a couple of steps closer to her. "You got my note."

"Of course I did." She cocked her head up at him.

"You read it that quick? It felt like I've been sitting here for seconds." His voice was opposite to the usual defensive tone he portrayed to Vira.

"Yeah, I guess I just..." She didn't even know what to say. "Am really eager to find this thing," she said, attempting to sound passive.

For a second, Cassius' naturally straight face turned into a grin. The single second, Vira found herself indulging in the rare sighting of the vampire's grin.

"So, what's going on?" he asked, going back to having a normal conversation.

"Hold on." She lifted up her pointer finger and then pulled out the two pages of the map, unwrinkling the pages and laying them flat on the bench. "These are the only possible places it would be." She looked up at him as she pointed to the bold circles.

Cassius bent down to look at the map. Vira watched his eyes roam the map, looking at the places she knew they needed to look so far.

"I was thinking we could start here first." Vira pointed to her late mother's former room. She had a feeling it would tear her apart when they did, but she guessed it would be best to get the toughest out of the way as well.

Cassius nodded, then noticed Vira's sudden closeness to him as her shoulder brushed onto his. He jerked back like he had seen someone coming and it startled him.

Vira's eyes grew wide in worry. She looked back to see nothing but darkness, not even the moon's shimmer breaking through the cracks in the trees above. But then she looked back at Cassius, and realized why his reaction happened. He was feet away from her now, still looking at the map. Vira's eyebrows drew in together in confusion and a bit of offense.

Cassius looked back up at her like nothing had even happened. But he did seem to pick up on her change of mood.

"What?" he asked cluelessly.

"Is there something wrong with me?" She held out her arms and flicked her eyes up and down them once in seriousness.

"No." He shook his head.

"Then why'd you move away from me like I had leprosy?" she asked, clearly upset.

Cassius seemed to just realize what he had done, like it was muscle memory, like he had done it involuntarily. But he did seem to feel guilty that he offended Vira.

"I…" he thought about it, "am sensitive to my personal space."

Vira cocked her head.

"Ever since I was in my double digits, I never knew how to be affectionate to people. I always felt odd being close to them," he explained.

"Ah," Vira nodded her head. "Makes sense." But really, she thought, *not really.*

She disregarded it, however, when she realized she shouldn't take it to heart and that it was, in fact, not personal. Now that she had realized it, she noticed how he would never let her stand within a foot's proximity of himself.

"So, the queen's room," he changed the subject purposefully as he continued to look down at the map.

"Yes, my mother's room," she clarified.

"Wouldn't she be asleep?" he asked.

Vira shook her head and sucked her lips into her mouth in an attempt to keep her emotions out of the way. "No, she's…" she took a deep breath and only managed to get out the single word, "Gone."

Cassius paused and glanced up at her in sorrow, then his eyebrows drew in together as he continued to look on the map.

It confused Vira, conflicting herself when she tried to decide if he was soulless, or how the vampire mind even worked. Perhaps, there was the possibility that he could be faking the emotion, but perhaps there could be something hiding deep down that every so often came up, which would explain the confusion. He lost everyone and Vira hadn't shown even a bit of sorrow thus far, yet he seemed to go soft every time Vira shared her traumatic side, she noticed.

Cassius had yet to say a word about it, though. His mouth stayed shut and he continued to look at the way of the map.

"I know exactly where it is," Vira broke the silence.

Cassius turned his head in her direction. "You do?"

"Yes, and I do get tired sometimes, just to remind you." She yawned.

Perhaps the vampire forgot not all immortals stay awake twenty four hours of the day.

"Ah," he nodded in realization. "So we better start heading there now."

"I agree."

She walked along the path leading outside of the secluded garden. She looked back when she noticed Cassius wasn't following behind her.

"It's dark enough." She smiled at him, which would be a first. "Come." She motioned him on.

His eyes glowed darker the closer he got to her. Once he was close enough, she turned around and walked all the way out of the garden

Luckily, most of the guards would be asleep by now and very few would be out walking. The back door would be a questionable place to enter the palace through, so they walked along the sides of the building until they reached the side door Vira had in mind, as it was closer to the queen's room anyway.

Cassius whispered to her, "You're sure we won't get caught?"

"We're only outside of the palace right now. I'll get a better view once we're inside," she explained.

Cassius seemed not to believe her the way he glared his eyes as he looked around paranoid. "Even if we do, is it really much of an issue?"

"Well..." She paused for a few seconds. Perhaps even she didn't know.

"I mean, wouldn't you be able to say you were just talking with me?" he asked.

"The queen's room. What would be our explanation for casually going in there?" she made a point of bringing it up.

"Well, you know this palace better than I do." He shrugged.

"I know, I've got it under control." Vira assured him that she would try and do her best to leave her foolishness behind and make sure they didn't get caught.

"It's my life that's on the line if I get caught," he stressed.

Vira sighed. "Perhaps you're right." But what seemed odd to Vira was the fact he all of a sudden cared for his life when not too long ago, he gave her permission to take his life herself.

"All you'd have as a consequence is some explaining to do," he said.

"Right, because I'd be caught helping you," she nodded her head. But what he didn't know was the sorcerer's oath, and that if she was caught with a literal vampire, her life would potentially be on the line right next to his. They'd have both of their heads at that.

"Yeah, so you better be careful. You never know what you'll be faced with. They could throw you out for all you know. You're not blood to anyone here. They don't have any obligations to you that way," he explained.

Cruel, Vira thought.

It stung Vira's heart to hear him talk, even if it was true. Suddenly, she had become sensitive to the fact that nobody in the palace really had her back.

"At least I have blood," she snapped back in an attempt to get under his ice cold skin just as he did hers.

"Ha ha," he fake laughed.

Vira placed her hand on the door knob as she peered into the room once they reached it. She opened it slowly and then looked back at Cassius, then said, "Vacant hall."

He nodded in response.

She slid swiftly through the doorway and held it open for him to do the same. It was a good thing nights at the palace were quiet and uneventful most times. Everyone would be sound asleep with the exception of a guard or two.

Vira mouthed *this way* as she pointed around the corner where her mother's old room would be headed. She remembered the last time she had walked down the hallway on the left wing. It would only be to visit her mother, as she pretty much had the premise all to her important self.

The feeling of loss and grief was already hitting Vira as old memories came to mind. She gulped to keep tears from flowing down her face. She couldn't tell if Cassius picked up on how emotional she was. He walked a step or two behind her, but she wasn't going to glance back at him to avoid him seeing her face. She read like a book and she knew it

At the end of the hall, they reached what would be the queen's room if there was one.

Vira took a step back from the door before placing her hand on the door knob. She took a deep breath before she turned it, then let it out once she opened it.

"Your mother was the queen, huh?" he asked.

"She was," Vira answered. "Normally, we won't call each other monarchical names, but my mother," she paused as she looked at Cassius, "was beyond queen-like."

The room had an old smell to it. Perhaps the servants felt the need not to clean it now that it was no longer in use. There even sat a small coat of dust upon many surfaces of the furniture. It was also twice the size of Vira's room, making it a potential all night search.

"We can't turn the light on," Vira whispered. "It will increase our chances of getting caught."

Cassius nodded as he looked around. Vira squinted her eyes as she let them adjust to the dark. Hung on the wall were displays of the crowns her mother had once worn.

Cassius went to the other side of the room while Vira stuck near the crowns. Perhaps it was better that the room was dark. It kept the memories from flooding in and making the search much longer than it needed to be.

Vira gazed at the shelf for a while in anticipation. She picked her tiara off of her head and compared it to them. It was tiny compared to the large, double-sized crowns. She glanced back at Cassius. He was way more focused than she was, and rightfully so. He had already made it through the entire dresser by the time Vira looked through the crowns of her deceased mother, realizing that she had seen her wear each and every one at some point. That gave her the sign that what Cassius was looking for wasn't where she thought. If it would be anywhere, it would have been with her other crowns as it seemed.

By now, Vira had guessed it to be that it wasn't in the room at all. She turned around again to tell Cassius. But just as she was about to, he was facing away from her, standing in front of the open closet. Vira's mouth opened, but no words came out. Cassius' hands rested on his hips as he gazed up in deep focus, looking at all of the shelves.

Vira didn't speak, still. It was half out of paranoia that even a whisper would attract someone to find them and half that she just couldn't turn her gaze from Cassius' direction. The guard uniform was tight from the waist down and the armor belt covered the front of his waist. Vampires were always said to be lanky but Cassius wasn't lanky. Perhaps it was her perception of vampires as a whole that made her believe they were all the same, and that they all had slim, frail features who were also pure evil and, over all, undesirable to anyone that wasn't of their kind. Perhaps the evil part was still in question, but the understanding that he was supposed to be undesirable melted from her judgment.

When she first laid eyes on him, she always thought the only desirable feature on him was the sculptedness of his face. But perhaps she was just never able to get a good enough look at him. For such an apparent arrogant jerk of a man whose guts were pure evil, he wasn't lanky. In fact, his figure was very sinewy. Perhaps the way he was standing contributed to his suddenly noticeable, muscular features through the leotard material.

He concluded his gaze and began to turn around. As he did, Vira quickly switched her gaze to look around aimlessly as if she was still looking as well. She was going to let him know this room had officially been ruled out, but suddenly, she wanted to spend more time with him, especially since she knew there wouldn't be much of it. The biggest prompt for her change of heart was her demand to figure him, and his feelings, out.

"It's not up here, I've checked," she motioned to the crowns. "But there's still more to look through," she bluffed.

"Where else would it be?" He held his hands up.

"The vanity." She pointed to it. "Every time my step dad finds something nice with diamonds on it, he brings it to her vanity in remembrance of her love for gems."

Cassius nodded.

But this time, they both headed to the area of the room. They reached the vanity at the same time, then Vira stepped back, remembering how Cassius didn't like being close to people. She watched him as he opened the vanity drawer where the jewelry would be. While he searched, Vira's emotions rolled in. It felt surreal to her that she hadn't been back to her own mother's room for years, and now that she was, she felt like a little girl again. Jewelry piled with gems all over hung from hinges. Much of the jewelry, Vira remembered her mother wearing, each and every piece, like it had all happened the night prior, and how beautiful she always thought it looked.

A single tear fell down Vira's cheek. She hadn't even been watching Cassius anymore, but he was, indeed, extensively searching through each and every piece of jewelry there was.

Vira knew one small tear was about to lead to several more, so she turned and made her way to her mother's still perfectly made bed. She sat on top of it and felt herself sinking down into the marshmallow-like comforter. Her cry hadn't made any noise, only tears had come. She had no energy left to let anything come out of her but tears.

Memories flood her mind just like she knew they would. There was one in particular of her mother telling her, *you'll always be the bestest to me, no matter what.* Even the improper grammar made it way more heartfelt than if it had been proper grammar. Maybe that's all she wanted was to be someone's *bestest,* even if it couldn't be her own mother anymore.

Vira sniffled in an attempt to control her crying, but that sounded through the silent room, causing Cassius to look back at her and notice her on the bed in tears.

He closed up the vanity and made his way to the bed and surprisingly sat next to her. He was still about a foot away from her, but that was also the closest they had ever been so far.

But Vira continued to silently sob as if he wasn't even there.

"I know," he whispered.

Her tears finally paused when he spoke and she turned her head to him.

"I know, it's like the world ends when someone you love leaves you," he added.

Vira nodded, then realized she knew nothing about Cassius. "I'm sorry, if…" she started.

"No," he held his hand toward her, "No apologizing."

"But I lost my mother years ago, and you…" She didn't want to continue on for the sake of his emotions.

"I can't cry," he said.

Vira looked up at him, then cocked her head. She could only see him as a blurry figure with the way her eyes were still filled up with tears.

"I can't cry because I haven't eaten a human in years, and we need blood to cry tears of blood. That's why I haven't been emotional," he explained.

"So, you…" She held a hand over her chest, unable to finish her sentence.

"If I was like you, at least some human, I'd cry until all the bodily fluids were absent, killing myself that way," he explained. "But yes, I'm holding it all in for the reason there's nothing I can let it out with."

"I feel," she shook her head then shifted to face him with her entire body before finishing her sentence, "Insensitive of you right now."

He gave her a look of confusion. "Why would you say that?"

"My mother passed away years ago and here I am, sobbing in front of someone who just lost everyone they ever knew and cared about." Her tears finally concluded.

Cassius shook his head. "Don't pity me, please," he said. "I'm trying way too hard to fit my narrative of being the cold blooded emotionless monster."

"Don't," Vira said, almost a little too loud. Once her eyes dried up, she no longer saw a blurred image of him, but his glowing skin complimented the dark and the darkness casted shadows upon his fine, sculpted features.

"Don't?" he asked.

"Don't call yourself that, please," she insisted. "I know it's hard not to take what people say about you seriously, but please, don't settle on what you think you are just because people have told you that's what you are."

"But what if it's what I'm destined to be? The villain?" he argued.

"No," she shook her head. "You are strong to come here and take back what was yours all alone from the island that defeated your entire family," she whispered extra quietly. "You've shown me how much worse it could be, and I really want to help you find this thing now so you can…" She choked on her words before saying them. "So you can go back to your island and live out the rest of forever."

Cassius was quiet for seconds in thought. Perhaps what Vira said changed his mind about his destiny. Something seemed to have clicked inside of his brain. But that was only what she had hoped. He was a stone iron soldier, which was enticing to Vira, but she didn't want to see him struck through the pain he was clearly hiding any longer, even if she had felt it too.

After a while, Cassius finally got up, but still said nothing to Vira. She squinted her eyes as she watched him open up her mother's vanity drawer again. He pulled something out and closed it back up again, but what he held was unclear to her vision.

He approached her from the front this time and took her hand and held it in his. It was like a breath of fresh air cooling down her warm palm in the areas his fingers touched it. He slid a thick, cuff-like bracelet lined with nothing but crystal jewels onto her wrist.

"Your mother would want you to keep this." He winked after he let go of her hand.

Vira looked down at the bracelet on her wrist. Now that she had gotten a better look at it, she recognized it as one of her mother's favorite things to wear.

"While I was looking around, my first thought was that it might compliment you well." His voice softened as he whispered. "And I was definitely right."

She looked up after letting out a small, uncontrollable giggle as the butterflies attempted to let loose, but she trapped them as best as she could. "Me? Look good in something to you? I'm atrocious to you." She playfully smiled.

Cassius giggled back and looked down as if he was blushing, even though it was near impossible for him to. "You're right. You're atrocious looking, even in that thing. It just adds a little something," he joked, agreeing with her.

But Vira blushed for real. The fire rumbled up inside of her and the sensation was new to her. It radiated through her veins, like a pleasurable feeling that hit all the right spots as the warm fire moved through her body.

"Well, looks like we at least got one thing done," he said. "We've ruled this room out."

"You're right, it's not in here." She nodded, shrugging her shoulders.

"Well, you better get to bed," he suggested. "Looks like we have some more to do tomorrow when dawn arrives, so you better head back to your room."

"That sounds like a good idea." Vira yawned even though the tired feeling hadn't even hit her entirely yet.

"Stay quiet." Cassius lifted a finger to his mouth as they made their way out of the room and he silently closed the door behind him.

It was a relief to shut the door without anyone else in sight. That meant their first mission had been completed, and only two more were to go. That meant, at minimum, there would be around two more days left for them to search the castle before they would find the crown.

Only one thing had changed from the beginning of the night, and that was whether Vira wondered if she wanted the quest to be over sooner or not. She thought for sure she'd want him gone soon enough, but now, she wasn't so sure. It was a battle against herself at this point.

THE LUNCHEON

S taying up late to search her mother's room left Vira exhausted the morning after. She didn't have much energy to do anything with the exception of working on painting her current work in progress.

By mid morning, she painted small lines in the scene with long red locks of hair. She started to paint a pair of black pants as well, but separated from the hair. She often wondered what it would be like to wear normal clothing other than ballgowns and other bulky clothes. She thought to ask for that in return for the quest, but it almost wouldn't seem worth it at that point. She still felt like she wasn't thinking big enough. Perhaps they got caught up in the emotional impact they both faced the night prior, which kept them from discussing what Vira would get out of the quest.

One thing dawned on her while painting, and that was the little things warmed her heart even more than anything wealth could bring her way, even despite being the step daughter of the ruler. As she painted the rest of the shirt above the black pants, it looked better to keep it plain white. Black and white complimented each other far more than she thought. Most of her painting was unplanned, both doing it and what ended up on the canvas.

By the time her arm had gotten numb from painting the morning away, another note from Cassius slipped through under the crack of her door.

She found it surprising that nobody had picked up on anything yet, but perhaps her step father's disregard for her continued to work to her benefit.

When she picked it up, an ear to ear smile spread across her face, which alarmed her because that hadn't ever happened before. Not with Cassius, not with anyone.

Vira,

I suppose we'd go to the exhibit holding room you circled. I say that because I observe that the safe is in the proximity of your step father's room, which should be our last resort since that's a dangerous place. What do you say, you meet me around there tonight? I have a general idea. Nobody has come up to me yet, which is an upgrade from yesterday, but it seems to be even harder to stay hidden. I've decided to fake sleep during the day and pretend to be nocturnal to avoid conversation at all costs and hope there's no palace rule against it. But no need to fret. Expect that this thing will be over by tomorrow. The light *at the end of the tunnel will come soon for both of us.*

-Cassius

A cold chill sensation flew down Vira's throat when she read the last two lines. She wondered if she wanted it to end at this point. She hoped she wasn't catching feelings for Cassius. That would not only throw everything off, but make everything a lot harder for her. It would ruin everything, really. But now she realized it was vain of her to hate herself for saving his life to begin with. After getting to know him as a person and not an enemy or an object, at least she could admitt to herself, she was glad she had saved him.

But she still felt like a charity service. He had yet to do anything for her, yet she had given him everything and more. He clearly hadn't felt the same way about her in terms of the note she read from him, but his words from yesterday confused her again. He admired her from what he implied, but he also shoved his feelings deep down into a bottomless pit of a vampire soul.

Vira now demanded to know his feelings for her, not just if he simply had emotions, because that answer had already revealed itself from the conversation the night prior. She decided she would make it a point to find out, sometime from now until he leaves back to Wintercastle.

The halls were nothing less than crowded this afternoon. As soon as she stepped foot outside of her room, she could see her step father approach her out of the corner of her eye.

"Vira!" he yelled over the chatter.

"Dad." She attempted to sound enthusiastic.

"I've been wondering about you," he said as he met her right outside her room. "I haven't heard from you."

Now, Vira fretted about him worrying about her. She was surprised he even seemed to care at all about what she had been up to. "Yeah," she fakely laughed. "I've just been relaxing," she lied.

"I haven't was worried about not seeing you yesterday. Come, join us for lunch," he offered. "It seems as though you've been checked out lately."

"Sure," she nodded. "I'd love to."

"Great, I'll see you there," he said and took off.

It must have been the weekend, as Vira would tell alone by the amount of people who were out.

Many of the guards were out, but none of them were wearing Aleski's uniform. It brought Vira peace of mind knowing that Cassius was hidden from the rather busy hour of the day, so he wouldn't even be in sight of anyone who might happen to take a closer look at him by chance.

She made her way through the crowded hallways to the dining room. For lunch, it was more of a buffet style. So she grabbed a plate, then stood in line.

"Vira," a familiar voice said behind her almost immediately after.

She glanced back to see who it was. It was Altha.

"Altha, hi." She smiled. "Joining us for lunch?"

"I am."

Altha didn't give off the same smile as Vira did. In fact it reminded Vira of her interaction with Cassius that she hadn't known about, and how Cassius said she may be onto him already.

"Great." Vira scooped a pinch of salad and set it onto her plate.

"You know, I don't hear from you like I used to," she said.

Vira didn't know how to respond, so she spent several seconds in awkward silence until Altha finally said, "Did you find your earring yet?"

Vira looked back up at Altha after she set a piece of pork onto her plate. "No, actually, I'm still looking for it." She nodded and forced a smile.

"Well that's too bad," she said as they approached the end of the line.

Vira sighed as she made her way to the chair closest to her step father. Altha ended up sitting across from her.

"Elvira, you came." Her step father seemed oddly delighted.

"Yes, glad to be here," she said over the chatter of the busy lunch room.

"So tell me, dear, what have you been up to?" he asked.

All Vira could think to do was compulsively lie. "Oh nothing out of the normal. I've gone to the courtyard a few times and stood by the stream. It calms me down."

"Ah, and how's that going?" He seemed to not know nor care what made her so uneasy to cause her to need to calm herself down.

"Oh, it's getting better. Memories of the war are fading by the day, and I'm feeling relieved," she explained, lying even more. She popped a piece of salad in her mouth to hide her guilt. Really, the war had very little to do with her uneasiness. It was more so the anxiousness of looking him in the face while lying, and maybe some confusion about Cassius as well. It scared her to know there was a possibility that she'd be into him.

"You know we won that war, right?" He seemed to want to wave her worries off.

"Yes, yes, just, a little traumatic for me still, that's all." She nodded.

"You'll look back and it'll be your favorite day soon, knowing all of the enemies are gone because of our joining with the wolves," he boasted.

Altha seemed to glance between both of them, yet acted like she hadn't listened to them by occasionally looking down towards her plate of food, poking at it.

Vira nervously laughed and said, "You're right, Dad." It hurt her to say the words.

"Ah, that reminds me, have you tried out your new meditation room?" He lifted a finger as he asked. "It'll help you with your powers and controlling them. Can't have another burnt servant."

"Yeah, actually, it works well." She hoped she wasn't being too cryptic, but she almost had to in order to avoid showing her true feelings. "I used it." She cleared her throat after she swallowed her food. "A few times, actually."

"Wow, marvelous," her step father responded, sounding pleased with her.

"Yeah." Vira fake smiled as she finished off her food.

"Well, Elvira, I'd like to see you come to more of these," he said. "We've missed you."

It wasn't even deep down that Vira knew his words were a lie. Not once had she been talked to at these dinners or even been asked to go to them. Perhaps it was only because he's on a happy wavelength, it would surely ride out soon. He'd go back to normal sometime soon, as Vira picked up on these common trends, and she wasn't fond of them. She never knew which step father she'd get. It would either be the one who wants nothing to do with her or the one who was bipolar to that. Either way, something still seemed insincere about the way he interacted with her.

"Sounds good," Vira said, wiping off a bit of the meat juice that had gotten on her face from the pork.

Altha seemed to keep an extra eye on her as she spoke to her step father at the lunch table. Not that she listened in to be nosy, but she surely was the first to notice something was going on with Vira.

Vira figured it would be worth it to confront her about it sooner, and maybe convince her to rule out any suspicions she had. Altha was intuitive and seemed to pick up on things easily. So she followed her into her office after a walk around the palace.

"Hey, Altha," she greeted her.

"Vira?" She seemed confused.

"Hey, how are you?" Vira tried to make casual conversation. "Sorry if you're busy with work right now, I just haven't gotten to talk to you in a long time."

She could see it in Altha's eyes that she had questions. The way her eyes studied Vira made her want to explode like a river with confession after confession.

"Yes, I was thinking the same thing," she replied. "You haven't been talkative lately, with anyone, really."

"Well, I don't know." She shook her head and sighed. "I guess ever since the war, I've been a little off."

"I could tell you're off, but are you sure it's still about the war?" she asked.

"Well, what else could it possibly be?" she asked.

Vira had hoped the answer wouldn't be something like *you tell me*.

But instead, Altha responded with, "Are you sure you're not a little..." She paused to think of a word. "Love sick?"

"Love sick?" she repeated a little too loud. She scoffed and looked around like it would give her an answer.

"Yeah, ever since the war and Jayden ending up with Ezri, you've seemed down about it," she explained.

It was a relief to hear that she had no serious suspicions just yet about Cassius and her.

"Oh," she paused, deciding whether or not she should just go with it or not. "Well, if I'm being honest, it seems as though everyone has been finding their love except for me."

Altha's face filled with sorrow. "I knew that was it."

"It's hard. Who am I supposed to be with?" She threw her hands in the air in an *I don't know* expression. "I mean, I didn't end up with any of the other sorcerers, I won't date one of the guards, and I surely won't date one of the servants. Other than that, I'm pretty much trapped up here in this palace, never to see the rest of what's out there."

Altha nodded. "When I started dating Zereck, I wondered if love just wasn't for me," she said.

"Really?" she asked, shocked.

"Yes. It was like everything tore us apart. But one day he told me he'd always find his way back to me no matter what it took. And he always did," she explained. "So when you find love, just know, it will always find its way back to you if it was meant to be."

Vira nodded. She agreed half way. However, those were the type of stories she'd hear in fairytales. But one thing different was that Zereck was a werewolf. They have a protection status that if they claim someone to protect, they can't go back and they won't have the physical or emotional strength to stay away from them.

Cassius was the polar opposite of Zereck, though, if he was the one. He was cold and wolves were warm. They also tended not to have feelings. Perhaps Altha had it different from her and she was only seeing the world through her own lens, as Vira thought.

"I see." She nodded in thought.

"So anyways, the moral of the story is not to search. It'll come." She ended the sentence with a smile.

"Right." She nodded. "I'll remember that, thanks."

"I'm glad," she responded.

"Well, I'll let you get on with your job, I'll come by again soon," she concluded as she started to walk out.

"Sounds like a plan," Altha said. "Good luck."

Vira turned around and waved again before walking all the way out of the office and into the hallway. She knew it would be hours before the night would arrive, so she headed back towards her room to catch up on some sleep before another tiring night of searching through the exhibit portion of the palace.

THE EXHIBIT

One out of three places had been ruled out so far where the crown could possibly be, and this night could possibly make two.

Vira set the paint palette to the side once the hallway chatter had stopped, indicating it was time for her to find Cassius again. The thrill snuck up on her once the night time had come.

The painting that sat in front of her now had a naturistic background and the woman she drew had legs and a head. It was still unidentifiable, but she liked the idea of creation and loved how it had come out so far.

As she washed the paint off the palette in the sink, she noticed her rather prominent feeling of calmness. Art felt inherently real to her, and not much did anymore. Being the ruler's daughter, she often felt that she had to put on an act for everyone, or maybe a mask was more accurate.

After she set the palette back down next to her now tucked away easel, she kicked her shoes off near her bed and cracked her door. She peeked outside into the hallway, as it seemed all the way clear and the premises were darker than dim. She pulled the map out of her dress and saw the artifact holding room to be near the far left wing of the palace.

Vira shoved it back into the pocket of her dress and headed down the hallway. It wasn't a far walk, luckily, so she'd be able to hide away if she needed to.

Once she turned the corner, Cassius almost startled her, the way he leaned against the wall impossibly still.

"Hey," he greeted her.

"Cassius," she said as she caught her breath after being startled.

"I told you I'd be here," he whispered.

"Good." She lifted a hand to her chest, catching her racing heart. "It's just down there." She noticed an object she could only make out as long, pale and skinny in his hand. "What do you have there?" She pointed to it.

"This?" He held it up. "You seemed to have had some trouble last night seeing in the dark. I thought I'd bring this for you to cast a flame on so you can see better."

Vira nodded and smiled. "Ah." She took it from him. "Thanks." She quietly laughed. "Stand back."

Vira focused her eyes on the opposite palm as she watched it heat up. A small flame rolled off of her pointer finger and onto the wick of the candlestick. She was surprised she was able to control it that time, and that she could do one thing successfully with her power.

The candle lit up a small portion of the hallway when Vira held it in front of her. They had the rest of the hallway to go before reaching the exhibit part of the palace, but Vira kept quiet until they approached the room.

All of the soon-to-be displayed items would be in a smaller room beyond a door next to it. Vira looked back and bobbed her head in the direction of the door.

Cassius leaned closer to Vira and whispered, "I'm going to go to the display room, maybe they've already taken care of it."

Vira answered with a head nod. She took a deep breath as she watched him walk into the exhibit. She placed her hand on the doorknob and turned it apprehensively. As soon as it cracked open, she could see the tiniest bit of light seep through the door from inside the room.

Vira assumed someone must have forgotten to turn off the light. So she opened the door the rest of the way to see a near elderly woman sorting through a bin of nick-nacks.

The woman gasped when she saw Vira, and Vira did the same.

"My, my," the woman held her hand to her chest in startle. "What brings you to stay up this late?"

Vira froze and glanced over to the exhibit room in a panic. But Cassius was nowhere to be seen, so her nerves settled some. He must have run off like he had the other day before anyone could see him.

Vira panicked and went with the narrative she had been going with all this time. "I…" She choked on her words. "I was trying to find my earring," she lied again.

"Your earring?" the woman asked.

"Yes, I was thinking it was in here."

"Ah, well." The woman looked around at the containers.

"I'd like to take a look, if you wouldn't mind," she asked. "It's red with golden detailing."

"Honey, I don't see an earring in here," the woman argued.

But Vira grew irritated that someone would keep her from ruling out the exhibit holding area when she knew she needed to.

"No, really, just let me real quick make sure," she demanded.

"Honey, I already told you I—"

Vira stepped further inside the room and held the candle up towards her head. The dim must have hidden her crown, but when she made the woman aware that she was the ruler's step daughter, the woman's facial expression changed to shock and guilt.

Vira's eyes glared at the woman to intimidate her. "It will just be a moment," she said.

The woman didn't say a word, stepping out of the way and moving to other containers.

Vira stepped closer to the artifacts on the table the woman had previously been looking through. Some were definitely from the war, as she found one of the vampire's teeth that must have been knocked out. The box was nearly empty, though, and not much was inside each one.

One by one, she rooted through each and every container, growing tired of the elder woman supervising her. At this point, she would be half glad if the crown wasn't in there.

Halfway down the row of boxes, her doubt grew that it wasn't in there, and that their last resort had to be where it was. But Vira could tell that not all of the vampire's valuables were in these containers. It was mainly clothing and vampire fangs. In fact, that's all there seemed to be.

By the time she reached the last container, it was enough to know it hadn't been ruled out yet. Vira's step father was known for keeping the valuables with him, anyways, so it should have seemed more realistic to begin with. But it was worth knowing, anyway.

Vira sighed as she retracted her hand from the last box.

The woman had a look of *I told you so,* but knew now to say it to Vira. She walked out without saying a word, then proceeded to blow the candle out. The first thing she needed to do was find Cassius and confront him that there was only one last possible place for the crown to be.

Vira knew Cassius wouldn't be happy about it, but what had to be done, had to be done, even if it would be the most difficult and daunting place to search.

Vira made her way to the secluded garden, as she had a sense that's where he would be. The night was rather dreary, but the cold temperature was worse.

"You came," he said as she caught his eye, pushing tree branches out of her way.

"I know you'd be here," she answered at the first sight of him.

"Give it to me straight." He seemed to already know what happened.

"Well, it wasn't in there. But maybe that was a good thing," she said.

"Why?" he cocked his head.

"There was a woman in the room watching my every move. She'd know I was taking the vampire's crown instead of an earring, which I said I was looking for," Vira explained.

"Ah," he nodded. "I fled once I heard her."

"Did you have a chance to look at all the exhibits?" she asked.

"Yes, and it wasn't there," he answered. "But maybe that's a good thing, too, considering they'd know it was gone from the display case if it was in there."

"Well, maybe ruling this one out really saved us more than we think," Vira realized.

"Yeah." He softened his voice. "Now, we know where it is now, at least."

"In my father's safe." Vira sighed.

"Yeah, about that, you may have to do that one on your own." He held his teeth together.

"I do?" she asked.

"Well, I can't run *that* fast. He'd catch at least a glimpse," he explained. "What if he wakes up?"

"I'll find his schedule tomorrow and see if I can catch him not in his room."

"Ah," Cassius nodded his head. "Good idea, princess," he said sarcastically.

"Princess?" Vira sounded offended.

"Aren't you a princess?" he asked.

"Well, I guess so…" She stumbled over her words. "I'm not sure, I…" She sighed. "I don't like princess." She laughed as she shook her head.

"Fine, Queen Vira," he said, clearly to pick on her.

"Who are you? Vampire Prince Cassius?" she stabbed back at him.

"No, I was never called that." He shook his head. "But if I got the chance to, I wouldn't have minded it." He stood up straighter. "Unlike you," he said with a smirk.

Vira didn't like being called princess. It was common knowledge at this point. She wore a tiara and deep red ballgowns and heels some of the time. She was only identified as a princess. But when she heard it, she'd cringe on the inside and try not to roll her eyes at anyone who did call her any type of monarchial name. It just didn't match who she really was. However, *Queen* was surely a new one. Surprisingly, she hadn't cringed on the inside when he called that.

"Yeah I guess I've just…" She gathered her thoughts to put them into words. But that was incomprehensible at this point, so she summarized and said, "Never really felt like I fit here."

"You haven't?" He seemed shocked.

"I guess I just feel like I don't belong sometimes." She walked over to the bench and seated herself.

"Why is that?" He sat next to her on the bench.

Vira realized then that she had never spoken of this before. She had a feeling of both letting go and apprehension. More so, it was strangest to her who she was sharing this side of her to.

"Well, none of my blood family is in my life, and my step father doesn't care to ever ask me how I'm doing nor does he care," she explained.

"Well, how *are* you doing?" he asked.

"Honestly?" Vira exhaled. "Not the best."

"I get that." Cassius folded his arms and relaxed himself. "Perhaps our situations are far more similar than we realize, Queen."

Vira swung her head over to Cassius in confusion. She almost didn't care at this point that he called her *queen*. "Really?"

"Well, is it better to have those who never cared for you, or have nobody at all, but once had tons who did?" he asked, comparing their scenarios.

"I'm glad more than anything to have once had my mother. Even if she left the earth when I was little, she still taught me a lot during that time. It's why I don't find importance based on hierarchy," she said after a moment of anticipating what Cassius said.

"Right." He nodded his head, seeming to take in what she said and admire it.

"I'm living in a palace full of strangers who don't care for my well being, or would care if I was okay," she ranted. "The memory of my mother is what I'm grateful for, way more than any of my acquaintances now."

"Was your mother beautiful?" he asked. Vira looked up at him, noticing a sparkling glare in his eye as he spoke.

"She was the most beautiful woman I've ever met." Vira's eyes grew teary.

Cassius looked straight ahead, gazing with a smile. Vira hadn't ever seen him smile before like he was now. More so, it felt like she hadn't seen him smile at all up until now.

"I bet," he agreed.

Vira couldn't decide whether he unintentionally called her beautiful or not, because Vira looked a lot like her mother aside from the tone of red her hair was, because that was adopted when she was given her power. She had also never seen a soft side of Cassius before, but it was worthwhile.

"You know, I don't know that I'm entirely comfortable with death anymore," Cassius said out of nowhere.

"Really?" Vira accidentally sounded confused. "That's great." She covered it up with excitement.

"Yeah, unless I get caught, which I'm counting on not happening," he added.

"You aren't scared of death?" she asked. She still wanted to know if vampires could feel things emotionally. More so, if he could.

"Well, it depends. I'm prone to not caring," he answered.

"What made you switch up?" She was curious to know.

"I don't think I know," he hesitated to say. He shook the subtle smile off of his face that seemed to try to force its way on.

"Well, maybe that's a good thing." She scooted an inch closer to him.

He turned his head in her direction on the bench without looking up, almost as if he was pondering something. Vira hoped it was moving over to take up the empty space that was between the two of them.

For a minute, they sat in complete silence. The only sounds were the whistling of the trees as the wind blew through them and Vira's small breaths. Really, she was trying to contain herself. The space between them seemed to get smaller and smaller every time they sat next to each other. Now, it seemed to get smaller and smaller every other second, at least it seemed that way for Vira. It seemed strange that he'd contradict what he said about personal space now that he seemed not to mind it more and more as time went on.

Oddly, Cassius unintentionally gave her a cold sensation without touching her. It wasn't unpleasant, in fact, it was the opposite for Vira. Normally, anyone else would describe their feelings for someone by comparing them to warmth. At least, that's how Altha would describe the feeling her wolf shifter boyfriend would give her since he was naturally warm. But Vira's insides were constantly naturally warm already, and Cassius' presence seemed to cool them down, leaving a pleasurable relief geeling. It was a new feeling for Vira, one she may have never known existed with a vampire unless she had become the sorcerer of flames. That, at least, had done one thing right for her.

"Well, I'm sure you're tired," Cassius interrupted the somehow unawkward silence. "You should go."

Really, Vira could stay out all night with him, even if it was just to sit near him.

"Are you sure?" she asked.

"You need your beauty sleep," he joked. "Queen Vira."

"Ah," she nodded. "I suppose that's why you look like…" She didn't know if her comment was too much of a jab back, but she stopped mid sentence just in case it was.

"You can't hurt my feelings," he said anyway. "But nice try. Now go." He pointed in the direction of the castle.

Vira rolled her eyes and stood up. She walked to the trees that led out of the secluded garden, then turned back to glance at Cassius one last time. Her heart thumped when she saw his eyes looking up at her in desire. She had expected him to be looking aimlessly around, or to the ground. But when she saw that his eyes were glued to her, she had a second of euphoric shock. She couldn't decide if he wanted to eat her or if he was admiring her the way his eyes were magnetized to her. But either way, she couldn't help but smile and let off a laughing scoff before she turned away to walk the rest of the way out of the garden.

The feeling she had gotten earlier from him persisted. Perhaps just the thought of him had brought a smile to her face and a new feeling to her chest that made her feel like she was floating, or like a breath of cold, fresh air, or maybe a little bit of both.

He was on her mind the entire walk back to her room. In some ways, she wished the night hadn't come to an end this fast. She almost felt robbed of her time with him. Perhaps now she wished she demanded that she stayed at the garden with him, whether she made up an excuse or not.

Vira hated even more that, soon, her time entirely would come to an end, because if she stayed with him long term, everyone would hate her and her life would ultimately be ruined. Nonetheless, it was never a part of the plan to begin with. But maybe now Vira hadn't cared so much about the plan anymore. She found falling asleep easier with the fantasies she created involuntairly in her head. She hated it and how she felt now.

THE SAFE

This time, the weight was only on Vira's shoulders. Only she had the ability to scope out her step father's schedule and take notes where he was and when. But she didn't know of such a schedule. She couldn't ask, nor could she observe.

Even when she woke up the next morning, flutters had still circled around Vira's stomach. Her first thought was Cassius when she woke up. Mainly because the last thing on her mind before she fell asleep was him as well. She knew for sure now she had grown an attachment to him, even if it was unintentional. But that made her even more determined to find the Vampire King's crown. It was important to him, which somehow meant it was important to her as well.

Thoughts of the last search wracked Vira's nerves as she sat in front of her vanity fixing her hair with the tiara and remembering not to put any earrings in her ears intentionally. She knew what her narrative would be if she had gotten caught by her father, which was why it would be best that she would go alone this time.

But she wasn't going to wait until the night arrived for this one, as the only definite time she knew her step father would be in her room would be when he was sleeping, even if he wasn't aware of his own surroundings. It was just too much of a risk. Vira had never seen the safe before. Perhaps she'd wake him just by handling it. He came off as a light sleeper. Either way, Vira didn't want to find out the hard way.

Hopefully for Vira, he'd be slightly foolish enough to leave her the key to unlock it. Or maybe he'd have the combination written down somewhere in his room.

Vira figured she'd take a casual stroll down the halls to stalk and pay attention to the door opening and closing of the room that belonged to her stepfather.

It bummed her she wouldn't have time to paint this morning, as everything had been moving fast and so did she, but she figured she'd come back to it this night, or the morning after. The easel was still tucked behind the vanity of her room and covered up with a towel from her bathroom.

She took one last look at it before she walked out of her room. This time, she actually wore her heels. She had to get used to them again and the ache they gave her feet when she walked in them first thing in the morning. Since ditching them because of the noise that would draw attention to her as she snuck around with Cassius at night, they were even more uncomfortable to walk in now.

She walked the opposite way she would normally go to the garden or the dining room to head near her step fathers room. A group of guards strutted the opposite direction of her. She continued to pass them, but she could feel one of them do a double take. She attempted to ignore it, but the feeling persisted. Her nerves went suddenly wild when one of them approached her.

"Vira," one of them called out and parted from the group to get to her.

Vira glanced at him, then looked over back at him again, pretending she just did not notice him. "Sorry." She laid a hand on her chest with a fake smile. "I guess I startle easily."

"Yeah," he said as they both stopped in the middle of the busy hallway. "Can I ask you something?"

Vira's stomach thumped. "Oh, sure."

"Aleski, he's been rather strangely quiet lately." Vira could tell he gave her a strange look even though his covering uniform when he asked.

"Ah, well, that's strange." She tried to keep her voice steady as she spoke.

"You wouldn't happen to know anything about that, would you?" he asked. "All of us guys have been wondering about it lately."

"No, I don't know what's going on." She shook her head.

"The man's not even following the schedule. He's been guarding at night and now he's sleeping in the bunks. He's also apparently got some weird sickness now that's turned him pale, and he doesn't care to get it fixed," the guard explained.

138

"Huh, he must be a tough man, then." Vira laughed. "Why don't I tell him in a little bit to switch his schedule back to normal."

"You can do that?" he asked, confused.

Vira stared at him blankly.

Then, the guard suddenly seemed to want to take back underestimating Vira.

"Sorry, I meant, thanks, madam." He gave her a small bow.

"Of course, now, I have something to take care of if you don't mind," she said, dismissing the conversation.

As soon as Vira turned around, her heart started racing again with unease that their time was running out and if they hadn't gotten Aleski to Kharmat soon, everything would be ruined. The plan would be destroyed and everyone would hate Vira's guts for what she did for a vampire man. She squeezed her wrist to try and calm herself down. She noticed her mothers bracelet still on her arm. She grabbed it instead, realizing it had helped some as she walked down the hallway.

It was a good thing the hallway seemed more and more crowded as she walked closer to her step father's room. That would be an indication she wouldn't be as noticeable creeping down the halls.

For a while, Vira stood behind one of the walls as she waited for something to happen within eyes' view of the door.

Vira's plan was to check the safe, assumingly find the king's crown, and then hide it in the fluff of her dress. It helped that her dress was thick enough to hide it, at least the one she had intentionally put on in the morning. Then, she'd wake up Aleski like she promised the guard. Well, really, she would pretend to wake Cassius up and somehow deliver the news of his crown being found.

The one thing she still hadn't worked through yet was how she'd explain how the crown went missing. Her guess was to play dumb, but she feared it wouldn't work the one time she needed it to.

The door opened and her step father strutted his way out of it. He looked into the crowd, causing Vira to hide further behind the wall so he wouldn't approach her.

As soon as she felt that enough time went by, she looked back out from the wall. He was nowhere to be seen, which was a good sign.

Vira made her way to his door casually and glanced back one last time. She slipped through it once she noticed nobody looked her way, and immediately shut the door behind herself. She took a deep breath to calm her nerves down before she opened her eyes to get to work since her time was limited.

The room was ginormous. She felt the pressure come when she glanced around frantically looking for a safe of some type. She pulled the map from her dress. From where she was standing, it had to be in his closet.

So she ran over to the closet and opened it up. His closet had to be half the size of Vira's room itself. But she still didn't know how to get into the large, metal safe. It took up half of the closet, so she didn't miss it. She ran to his nightstand and quickly opened up all the drawers in search of the code. In return, she found nothing. She slammed the last drawer she looked through and turned away to face the safe again. It was now that it hit her that what she was doing was criminal. It was of no great taste, more so.

The safe had a number pad on in order to get into it, so she at least knew it was a code of some type. She panicked and pressed his birthday, which was March the third. The big button at the bottom lit up red. Then, she tried her birthday, which was June the twelfth. The button lit up red again.

Vira was in the midst of gathering all of the number combinations it could possibly be when the doorknob jiggled. Her heart stopped as soon as the door opened. She didn't know whether to come clean, hide, or pass out on the floor and pretend she had just gone insane. But she couldn't decide, so she just froze.

She turned around slowly with her eyes wide. Her step father hadn't noticed her right away, but as soon as he turned back from hanging his coat on a hanger, his screams echoed through the entire room. Vira felt the need to scream too, just in fear of what her worst nightmare had now become.

"Vira?" he yelled. "What are you doing?"

She moved away from the safe. When she did, he seemed even more confused.

But Vira remained silent. Her entire body was still paralyzed with fear and shock.

"Uh," she managed to mutter. The more she tried to speak, the more she felt that it would come out as vomit instead.

"Explain yourself, now." He had never sounded as upset with her as he was now.

Vira gulped and said, "I lost an earring during the war." She held her stomach as it nervously gurgled. "And

I thought it might be in here, as Altha told me we had it all."

Her stepfather's face faded into relief, and soon after so did Vira's. It felt like she had just caught herself after falling off a cliff.

"Well, why didn't you just say so?" He smiled. "Here, let's look for it."

Vira's stomach settled and she smiled as she said, "Yeah, thanks, Dad."

He pushed past her and stood in front of the safe. She saw him dial the numbers seven-seven-three-four. She mouthed it to herself, then said it three times in her head so she'd remember it for later if she needed to. At least one thing good came of her getting caught sneaking into it.

Once the safe opened, it looked even bigger inside than it did on the outside. Piles of diamonds sat all over, and jewelry galore had been stacked on top of each other, some intertwined with the diamonds.

Vira stepped closer to get a better view of the valuables that were in the safe. For sure, some of the vampire's valuables were stacked inside. They had to belong to them, as Vira could just tell by the way they looked far more gothic than anyone in the entire palace was.

"What does it look like?" her step father asked.

Vira peered deeper into the safe as he began rummaging through it and said, "It's deep red with golden detailing."

"Ah, I think I know which one you're talking about," he responded.

Thank goodness, Vira thought. She wasn't even sure she actually owned an earring of that description, but she was glad he at least followed her narrative.

"I'll help you look," he answered.

Vira's eyes clamped shut in annoyance.

Of course, she thought.

Now, she dreaded the entire search, because now it had come down to this. The way he invested himself deeply into searching for the nonexistent earring made her feel that it would never get anywhere.

As her stepfather moved the diamonds around, something big and black caught Vira's eye. She immediately reached her arm in the safe to uncover the rest of it. It was, indeed, a crown. It was made of thick black metal and had small, white and red jewels interspersed throughout the valley of it. It was round and rooney, wide enough to fit the head of a man. It had to have been the king's crown, as it had been the only crown in the entire palace taken back from them.

Vira noticed the hand she extended into the safe caught his attention. He eyed it up immensely. Vira couldn't understand why until she retracted her arm, realizing her mother's bracelet was still on her wrist. She put her hand over it as if it would make him forget about it.

"Is that your mother's?" he asked, like it was offensive.

"Yeah," she nodded. It wasn't worth lying about this time. "I've just been missing her. I thought having something of hers would help."

"You haven't gone into your mother's room in years," he observed.

Vira sighed and said, "Yeah."

Her eye was still on the crown that was now exposed right in front of her face. It took everything in her not to grab it and run away. She would have waited until he wasn't looking to snatch it and hide it in her dress, but her step father was way too observant. At least she knew right where it was, and the code to unlock the safe. It all started to feel like she could see it coming to a near end, just slower yet faster at the same time than she would have liked.

"Well, darling." Her step father shoved the rest of the diamonds to the back of the safe and said, "I believe that's all we have."

"So we don't have it?" Vira asked, filling her voice with fake sorrow.

"I'm afraid not." He shook his head. "I'm sorry."

"No, really, it's okay." She shook her head. At least now she knew how to get into the safe and what the crown looked like. Perhaps she would just have to come back another time.

Vira walked out of the room back into the crowded hallway without any further conversation after the safe had been closed back up. The people who walked around seemed to mind their own business, so she guessed it would be a rather good time to find Cassius and confront him. One more day should do the trick. But it was more of a question of when she'd be able to sneak her way back into her step father's room. The next time had to be perfect,, or else she'd be done for.

More guards walked the halls, meaning there wouldn't be many guards back in the bunk room. As she made her way past the door to the room that housed the guards, she couldn't quite catch a glimpse of Cassius yet.

It was a maze to get through all of the people blocking her view walking straight when she was trying to get across the hallway.

When she walked inside the guard room, she paused to take a breath.

"Aleski," she called out.

Cassius opened his eyes. Luckily there were only a couple of guards still in the room.

"Why aren't you walking the palace?" she asked. "We need you at the back."

"Ah." He stood up. "Didn't know I couldn't be nocturnal."

Vira, by no means, wanted Cassius to have to pace the halls. But if that's what it meant to keep people from being suspicious of them working together, then she would do it.

They walked the halls far enough apart that nobody would know they were talking to each other.

"Your guard friend yelled at me this morning, telling me to tell you to stay on schedule," she explained. "Sorry."

"Didn't know there was a schedule," he whispered.

"Stay wherever you'd like, though." She smiled, as they both knew where he would be.

Although she wanted to avoid talking to him with anyone around at all, it just had to be done at this point. One time wouldn't hurt.

"I'll walk you there," she lowered her voice.

Cassius simply nodded.

As they walked the halls, she stood far to the left of him. They didn't say much, but the chemistry between them had surely changed since the last time they walked the halls. They were business partners, but there was also something emotional now. For an ice cold vampire without a beating heart, he sure did make Vira's heart beat hard enough for the both of them.

They made it to the one place in the back of the palace they knew they would be least likely to get caught.

"What happened?" Cassius said as soon as he slid behind the wall with his back flush to it.

Vira sighed as she said, "Well, I found it."

Cassius lit up. And by lit up, he faintly smiled, which was his version of lighting up.

"But my step father watched me the entire time," she broke the news. "So I don't actually have it yet, but I know where to get it."

"Ah, so, you'll still get it."

"I will," Vira nodded. "Just sit tight."

"Anyways, I better get back to—" As soon as Vira stepped back from the wall, her sentence was interrupted by her name being called.

"Vira!" the voice yelled.

Vira froze, eyes wide as she slowly searched for the voice who had called her name. It was Altha.

When Altha saw that Aleski, who was really Cassius, was there too, her eyes grew wide. At that point, everyone's eyes were wide.

Altha paused once she gathered something was clearly going on.

"Catch you later, stranger," Vira said to Cassius as she fast walked to Altha.

Vira clearly had some explaining to do. Only, she didn't have a lot of time to come up with an explanation.

"Uh…" Altha struggled to even decide what to ask. "What was going on there?"

Vira noticed she had now been making her way back to the Altha's office alongside her.

"Oh, I just…" Vira still didn't know what to say. Instead, she didn't say anything. Her face stayed still and her pulse grew.

"I know exactly what is going on now," she said, motioning into her office.

"You do?" Vira gulped.

"Yes," Altha said as she nearly slammed her door shut, making Vira flinch.

She shook to the core as Altha walked in front of her suspiciously.

"You have a thing for one of the guards," she suddenly boasted. Vira had never seen someone's facial expression go from suspicious to excited that fast.

"Ah," Vira nodded her head as if it was news to her. "I mean, ah, yes." She nodded her head again. "You caught me, I surrender."

The relief settled in as Vira continued to just go with it.

"How could you not tell me this? I thought we were friends." Altha sounded offended yet gushy at the same time.

"I guess I just…" Vira sighed. "Wanted to keep it a secret." She shrugged.

"Which one is he?" Altha was eager to know.

"Aleski," she continued to bluff.

Altha froze as she said, "Isn't he like ten years older than you?" She seemed half grossed out.

Vira hesitated to nod. "Yes, that's why I didn't want to tell anyone quite yet." She laughed nervously.

"I see." Altha nodded slowly.

"Yeah, I guess I just wanted love." Vira sighed. "And besides, I'm in my twenties. It may be taboo, but older men seem to attract me now."

"You're right." Altha finally laid off on judging her. "I guess the mid thirties aren't too awful. I mean, Zereck's approaching the big three-o."

Vira smiled as she said, "Right."

"Well, I might as well let you get back to your day. I'm sure you have plenty to do." Altha smirked.

"Yeah, you're right." Vira fake smiled.

Really, Altha had no idea what she had going on with the rest of her day.

"I'll see you."

"Let me know how it goes for you two," Altha concluded.

Vira looked back just before she walked out and said, "Of course."

Vira held her chest and exhaled a sigh of relief as she left the premises of Altha's office. Maybe Altha had her back more than she realized. Although, a guard in his thirties is nowhere near as juicy yet shocking as a vampire who's been alive since the ancient years.

Vira had enough of the eyes and ears of the palace's hallway, so she headed back to her room. She didn't know what Cassius was up to, but she figured if anything were to go down, she'd be able to know even from her room.

Vira pulled off her dress and slid on her robe. Then, she kicked off her shoes and pushed them under her bed. She found herself in front of the canvas she had still been painting.

Thoughts of the earlier incident still pondered her mind as she sat down to paint small details of the body figures she was working on. She wondered when she'd be able to visit her step father's vault without the fear of him catching her breaking in again. If she was right once, she'd never get caught. It was make or break for her at that point. The pressure would entirely be on her, too, even if Cassius would be brought down with her. If that happened, she knew how it would end. Cassius would die for once and for all, and they'd force Vira to be the one to light him on fire. But at that, she didn't know if she'd be physically able to. And if that happened, Vira may just be homeless and sucked of both her powers and memory at that point by the Kharmat snake.

Nonetheless the thoughts didn't stop her just yet. Half of them told her she could turn everything around at any time, and the other half told her she was too deep into the plan already to break it off. Surely if she had gotten this far, she'd be able to make it work. It was the light at the end of the tunnel that kept her going as it got bigger. Surely she'd be able to scope out her step father's schedule in order to map up a plan to go into his room and retrieve the crown.

But one thing left Vira feeling blue, she couldn't quite pinpoint it. It was a new feeling for her that she couldn't quite process. More so, she hadn't processed the feeling since her mother passed away. All she knew was it had something to do with the adventure coming to an end. Perhaps it was Cassius leaving. Perhaps it was having someone to talk to other than Altha. A man. A surprisingly, seemingly sympathetic, relatable man who also happened to be the enemy.

One thing stuck out to her, though. She hadn't received a note from him yet. Perhaps there were just too many people out and about in the halls, which was normal for this time of the day. But it seemed to settle as she was near the end of the painting. In fact, her room had almost entirely dimmed, syncing with the outside lighting. Perhaps more time passed than she expected as she sat painting.

After Vira rinsed her paint palette one last time, she grabbed the tea cup and raised it to her mouth to sip. She then took the butterscotch cookie that sat on the plate next to it and took a bite. She didn't realize she hadn't eaten since the morning breakfast one of the servants brought to her bed.

Vira gazed at the beautiful, now finished painting as she took another bite of her cookie. It was of a man and a woman, and what she seemed to wish she could have. She would normally paint how she felt, displaying her inner, subconscious thoughts. But she continued to look deeper into the painting. The couple was laying on a grassy field or what could be interpreted as a naturalistic setting looking into each other's eyes, indulging in each other's presence. It would be a dream come true for Vira to look at a man like that, and to have him look at her like that, and for her to feel true love. Maybe that's why she made the woman look similar to herself. Mainly because she painted her to have deep red hair as Vira's and her dress was a light sundress, much less of a ballgown than she was used to. But once Vira observed that part of the painting, she squinted her eyes at the man in the picture. She drew him to have black pants and a white dress top. His hair was somewhat messy, yet strangely put together, shaded somewhere between an ash and golden brown color. His face was lighter than hers, giving off a subtle glow. Perhaps she hadn't realized it, but she drew...

Vira nearly choked as she swallowed the cookie she had been chewing on as she realized, *Cassius!*

It was, indeed, him, just how she remembered him the first time she had ever seen him. Perhaps she didn't grasp it right away because he hadn't looked like himself the past several days covered up in the guard uniform. But it *was* him. All this time, she wondered how she had gotten such inspiration for the man she had drawn in the picture, but now she knew.

Her mouth stayed open in shock after she sipped her tea to clear her throat of the cookie chunk.

Vira's face still filled with shock and some terror as she backed away from the painting to sit on her bed in deep anticipation. She wanted Cassius. Perhaps for more than just the mission. It was clear that was the cause behind the feeling of dread she got that it was all coming to an end soon. And perhaps, she also knew she couldn't confess the feeling she knew she had.

She wondered, though, why it had to be with someone that was her complete opposite. She was made of fire and he was the ice to the core. They were natural enemies who would always want to kill each other. She even tried to kill him, but somehow ended up saving him, all because he attempted to kill her first. She liked the idea of killing him, then when she found out she didn't kill him, she still wanted to kill him. She knew she should have listened to Altha. But she would only continue to take her advice, and if it was meant to be, they would always find their way back to each other.

Vira tucked herself under the blankets of her bed as she finished off the last bite of the cookie. She closed her eyes, and when she did, she saw Cassius in her dreams approaching her in slow motion in black pants and the enticing white dress shirt with less of the buttons buttoned this time than when she once saw him in at his first approach. It was almost an envisioning of the first time they met, reimagined how it should have gone. But this time, the subtle smile he would always try to hide was what she had seen and just the right amount of sunlight hit him as he gleamed with a tiny crystal type glimmer on his skin.

She reached out to him, feeling her heartbeat, radiating a euphoric feeling of desiring him every step he came closer. He slowed down to her. She caught a glimpse of sparkle in his eyes as he looked into hers. He reached out to her, the first time she would ever touch his hand. Even that seemed like a desirable privilege to her, as she knew by now that he always avoided skin contact.

But night had other plans shortly after Vira had fallen asleep. Vira felt like she had abruptly woken from a nightmare, her pulse racing as she tried to catch her breath. She sat up and caught a glimpse of nothing but a pair of glowing eyes. She held onto her blanket tight to control herself just enough not to scream at whatever kind of monster figure had entered her room as she slept.

IN THE DARK

Vira shook her head vigorously and rubbed her eyes, noticing that the eyes had disappeared. It was a shame she had to wake up just before the best part of the dream.

The room was pitch black. Even Vira's natural, bodily fire glow was put out. She startled when she felt a small touch of a cold sensation poke her arm. For a second, she felt like she was having a heart attack.

"Who…" she stuttered. "Who's there?" she said as her voice filled with utter fear.

"Relax, princess queen," a low voice said. "It's me," the deep voice whispered in her ear along with a cold sensation, like he was holding ice near it.

Vira screamed as the words startled her.

Less than thirty seconds went by of her hyperventilating when the door opened and light peered into the room from the hallway.

"Darling?" It was her step father who opened the door. "Are you alright?"

Vira still held her hand to her chest as she calmed down. "Yes, I…" She frantically glanced around to see nothing at all. "I think I had a nightmare."

Her stepfather nodded and said, "Alright, you best be going back to bed now."

Vira knew it wasn't the fact that she had a nightmare that concerned her step father; it was the scream that woke him up. The way he dismissed it was no surprise.

"Alright," Vira nodded. "Sounds good."

"Nighty night," he said before he shut the door again and left.

Vira rolled her eyes as she brushed her hair back out of her face with her fingernails. She knew what she saw, and knew there had to be something or someone near. But when the door was shut, it was now pitch black again.

But now that she had a moment to breathe and think straight, she knew there had only been one person in the entire world to ever call her *princess* or *queen*. And at that, a smile grew on her face slowly.

Her eyes adjusted to the dark and when she looked over, she knew better than to be startled at a figure standing tall, leaning against the wall next to her closet. It was an indent in her room that wouldn't be seen from the door.

Vira pushed herself off of her bed and squinted her eyes as she walked closer to the figure, who she now knew was none other than Cassius. She didn't know whether to speak to him or not even say a word. But when she got close enough to him, it was like her dream came true. She saw a faint figure of his arm extend to her, grabbing by her fingers, leading her gently closer to him. The closer she got to his flesh, the more the pleasurable cold sensation touched on her skin, even if she wasn't touching him yet other than the tips of his two fingers.

All Vira could feel at first were his hands chilled touching hers. His fingertips released from her hand, then began to brush up her arm, enticing her warm skin, giving her chills in a good way. She thought maybe this was his way of bringing on the temptation. Either way, the fact that he had actually touched her meant something special. She wondered for a moment if she was the first one he had touched out of intimacy. All of a sudden, she decided that it couldn't have been only to tempt her more to get the crown. There was no way he could go that far to do something he'd otherwise despise.

The darkness got even darker to the point she could only feel, not see, like her eyes were closed. A cold breath landed upon the side of her neck, causing her to lengthen then arch it to make it more accessible.

Soon, she found it was only to whisper in her ear, "Fake sleeping for eight hours listening to the snoring of ten other guards was driving me insane."

Vira softly laughed as a response.

"I couldn't stand another minute inside that room," he whispered again.

After he spoke, Vira didn't respond. Mainly because immediately after, she felt his fresh, cold breath travel down her neck again. As his mouth got closer and his breath got harder, so did hers.

Her hands still hung loose at this point. But when his breath got even closer to her, she felt his lips softly touch the side of her neck. All that was touching her were his lips.

Vira felt like fireworks went off inside her. She had no idea why he would suddenly kiss her and it didn't even make any sense. But it didn't matter to her. Even if all this time prior to the painting he was the last person she'd think to kiss, it was nothing less than enjoyable.

"You don't know how bad I've wanted to do this." She couldn't help but smile again.

His lips lifted from her neck so he could whisper into her ear, "You don't know how bad I want to do more."

Vira lifted her hands, feeling around until she grabbed the sides of his face as she moved her head to his, his mouth hanging by her neck yet again when she asked, "What do you mean? Suck the warm blood out of me?" She chuckled. She knew what vampires wanted most of the time, and the fact that he seemed to focus only on her neck made her believe that's what he meant. "My friend Altha can help you with that if you're craving blood," she joked. Vira didn't really have blood. She had fire veins. But Altha had a healing flower that universally donated blood.

Vira heard his voice close again to her ear, hearing him laugh quietly.

Chills were not just on her arms now, but everything had the same pleasurable sensation. It had become apparent Cassius felt the need to call her *queen*, which seemed peculiar, considering Vira was no queen.

"Feisty Fire Queen," he joked.

"Flame Princess," Vira said back to him. "If you're going to call me anything monarchical, that is."

A slight chuckle came from Cassius' mouth just before he then kissed Vira's jaw gently, then kept going, working his way up near her ear and demandingly whispering, "Don't tell me what to do."

"That's too bad," Vira answered.

She was growing tired of the teasing. She could only feel his face, and continued to pull it closer to hers. He was the one against the wall, so that ultimately meant she was in control. She should have known her thirst would get the best of her.

He willingly let her bring his face closer to hers. She only knew that she was pulling it forward. But she didn't know where his lips were. So she froze, worried that she'd embarrass herself by kissing his nose or accidentally slobbering on his chin.

Yet she knew he could see far better in the dark than she could, so she proceeded to say, "Kiss me." Her voice grew demanding. "Now."

"I would normally tell you not to tell me what to do, but I'll let this one fly."

Vira held still as he wrapped his chilled lips around hers like a glass of ice cold water on a hot summer day. She arched her body up on him as the kiss grew passionate, letting her body go flesh to his as she felt his arms wrap all the way around her torso.

Every second was euphoric for her up until her breath got denser and she clung onto him extra tight, moving her hands around his neck and shoulders. It was already too late when she had felt her palms heat up all the way out of passion. She let go of him, pushing herself back from him just in time for flames from both hands to roll off her fingers, startling them both.

That concluded the end of the romantic moment. She could no longer feel Cassius on her at all. She held her hands together with a look of sorrow and lousiness.

She sighed. She couldn't believe she had just ruined the moment.

"Nice try," she heard his voice say as a joke. It was more so to turn it lighter, much less than he actually believed she actually wanted to hurt him with her flames.

Luckily, it wasn't enough to set anything on fire, or burn anything.

"I should probably go to bed," she said with doubt. "I don't want my step father coming in again."

"Good night, Cassius," Vira said as she crawled back into bed after finding it with her hand.

"I'm right here." His voice was close enough to know he was right next to her already.

Vira already felt better that he wanted to stick with her even after the flame incident, leaving an ear to ear grin to form on her face. She made a flame with her finger to see her way around. She leaned right to light up a small candle that sat on her nightstand. Once it was burning , her eyes could adjust to see at least a better image of him.

She leaned down onto her bed, still looking at him as she said, "I'm working on figuring out what I'm going to do next."

"Next?" he asked.

Vira proceeded to ramble. "Yes, I know the combination of the safe. I just have to find out his schedule so I know when he comes out of his room and for how long. I'll also somehow see if I can get any info from the guards. Who knows? Maybe you'll be able to go in, maybe it's normal for guards to go into the safe."

"Vira." He sounded demanding. "For once, take a break. You're only ever worried about focusing on me and what I want nowadays."

"Oh, I am?" she asked.

She considered it, realizing he was right. She never had any time for herself anymore other than when she was painting, and even that was more so about him instead of her, even if she didn't see it that way at first.

"That's why I kissed you," he said softly as he leaned down on the bed, relaxing himself, looking into her eyes.

Vira smiled uncontrollably again as the fluttering feeling went wild throughout her entire body.

"Hey, I was wondering," Vira said. "Why did you say you *wish* you could do more?"

"Well, If a human, or other being, has a baby with a vampire, it'll end badly," he explained, nodding.

"End badly?" she asked.

"People have died, demon babies were born, who knows what else," he replied.

"Ah," she sighed. "Interesting," she said, sounding underwhelmed.

"And because I don't want to be attached to you anymore than I already am," he added.

Vira looked down, disheartened as she said, "Ah."

The silence confused her some, the way he looked at her with the same desirable stare from the night before.

He then interrupted the silence with, "You know, I can't see you well, but you've never looked this beautiful before, Queen Vira."

Vira's eyebrows drew in together and she playfully slapped his cheek.

"No," Cassius laughed as he moved her hand away from his face and explained. "I mean, maybe you've made me believe that there's someone on this planet worth bleeding out for."

Vira looked up at him again, this time in even more shock. "Bleeding out?" she asked, confused.

"See, uh." He smiled. "I was a human once, too, before I was a vampire. I thought I was going to die. One of my organs bursted inside of me and they didn't have the proper medical equipment to save me back then. That was one of the reasons I opted to become a vampire, and the king sucked me of all of my blood so I could live on."

Vira's eyes were wide as she said, "Wow." She nodded. "That's a story." She also noticed how he said it was only *one* of the reasons, making her wonder how many more there were.

"But it's not all easy, especially not now, since I'm the last one left," he added.

"Yeah, I'd imagine." she sighed. "I feel like anywhere I go, I don't belong. I'm in this constant state of misplacement."

"You'll fit in somewhere, even if it is nowhere," he answered sarcastically.

"That made no sense," Vira said as she rolled on her back and looked up at the ceiling. "Be careful, I'll kill you. I know how to now."

"I'd love that," he responded with a smirk.

Vira closed her eyes with a smile as she dozed off, hoping he'd be right there in the morning. The only worry on her mind was that somehow it would all have all been a dream as breathtaking as it was.

MISSING

Vira's eyes fluttered as soon as she had woken up from the light of the morning cracking through her eyelids.

A smile had stayed on her face from the night prior. But she opened her eyes, and Cassius was, in fact, not in the same place she had last seen him. He was nowhere to be seen at all.

She shot up out of her bed and slid on her heels. She pulled a random ball gown dress from her closet and worked it over her head to put it on the rest of her body.

Her feelings for Cassius were solidified; they could not be undone. Losing him one way or another would ultimately shatter her life, leaving her to live a long, depressing episode for the rest of time.

Something seemed off about him leaving, though. If she knew anything about him by now, it would be that, as much smack talk as he gave her, the more he didn't mean it, and the more it really meant he actually wanted her, like he had mentioned the night prior.

Vira would much rather have preferred him to be her first sighing as she awoke, but for one reason or another, he had other plans.

Naturally, she wondered if the night prior was all a dream from her feelings after she finished the painting. But it was so lively, it seemed impossible.

Vira left her room on the search to at least find him. The first place she'd look was the back door where he'd normally pretend to guard to avoid interaction.

She strolled casually through the halls, but made a point to walk at a rather fast pace, eager to find him. She stopped at the back door and looked around frantically.

He was nowhere to be seen. A burning feeling started in her chest. It was half worry and half anger. He told her he would be there when she woke up. Something could have either happened to him, or he could have betrayed her.

So Vira headed towards the guards' bunk rooms. She had hoped as she made her way through the crowd that it hadn't seemed apparent that she was looking for someone or up to something.

Once she made her way through the halls, yet again passing through the group of crowded people, she still hadn't seen him when she poked her head into the guard's bunk room.

Cassius was nowhere to be seen at this point, and she wondered if she'd see him come around at some point in the day. So she decided to walk the halls around the palace several times. Surely she'd see him somewhere and surely she was just over reacting. There was no way he had gotten caught, or else everyone would have known it by now, and she'd be the first one to know.

It had been hours, and Vira had paced the halls of the palace at least three times. The palace was a ginormous place, which meant she was out of breath by the time she had gone around.

Her step father caught her eye, looking like he was discussing something important with a suited man she hadn't recognized. It was pretty normal stature for him, but Vira guessed it would be a good idea to listen around at what may have been the reason she hadn't seen Cassius yet.

The servants were already bringing out plates of food and setting them on the round tables with beige tablecloths.

Vira walked over to it and grabbed one.

It was a maze to get through the crowded room and find a seat next to her step father, who was still talking to the man she had seen.

He glanced at her, then looked back at her when he noticed she had taken a seat surprisingly.

"Vira." He held his hands up as if he disbelieved it. "You've come."

"Yeah, I guess I just wanted to spend time with you," she responded.

The man he was talking to walked away, finding a seat next to another man who then started a conversation to give Vira and her step father privacy.

Surely with the normalcy going on around the scene, there was no way Cassius had gotten caught yet.

"So, how has everything been going in the palace after the war?" she asked.

"Ah," he patted the corner of his mouth with a napkin and continued, "Better than ever." He smiled.

"I see." Vira fake smiled as she nodded. She shoved a forkful of food in her mouth to keep her from acting unnatural and giving herself away to be questioned.

"Have you seen the new flower garden?" he asked with a smile.

Vira almost choked on her food. She pounded her chest and took a sip of water to contain herself. When she could talk again, she asked, "Which one?"

"The courtyard." His smile persisted. In fact, it almost seemed creepy to Vira the way it was painted on his face like a clown's smile.

"Ah," she answered, underwhelmed. "It's nice," she struggled to say.

"Isn't it?" he arrogantly answered.

The conversation only reminded Vira of how greedy she felt when she saw Altha's flowers as the replacement, taking over the courtyard. Vira looked around, and yet again felt lousy about not being appreciative of what she had. She was a princess, and still wanted more than she was given, even if she didn't know what it was that she wanted.

The toughest part was that she knew Altha needed the sorcery flowers. She came from deep poverty in search of a better life, and she deserved it for as hard as she worked.

Seconds went by and Vira was silent from the feeling she got when she acknowledged the courtyard. The anticipation was deep enough to make her forget that she was still eating and when she set her fork back on top of the plate, it was nearly empty and Vira then had no appetite left. Her stepfather hadn't said a word either, but had a look of confusion, most likely in wonder of why Vira got quiet when he had mentioned the courtyard.

But Vira got all the information that she needed. She knew now that there was nothing going on in terms of Cassius. So she figured she would get back up to search the halls, while she appeared to leisurely stroll.

"I expect to see you again soon," her step father said after Vira had gotten up to drop her plate in the depositary.

"Of course." Vira didn't mean to sound insincere and underwhelmed when she spoke. But she gave a fake smile and nod to cover it up before she made her way back to the hallway.

Her step father waved slightly with one hand.

There had still been one place Vira hadn't checked yet, and that was outside. So she headed towards the back to see if there had been any sign of him.

She wondered now if what happened between them the night prior had been a dream. It would make sense, after she had finished her painting, therefore coming to terms with her feelings for him. And she had been helping him a lot, more than herself. So perhaps she had dreamed the exact thing she craved to hear from him.

The outdoor breeze brushed over Vira, chilling her entire body which reminded her of Cassius. But still, he was nowhere to be seen. She pondered for a moment if she had just gone delusional, and that the chilling feeling from her body had only been from the breeze, and Cassius hadn't existed at all, and perhaps, in her dream she felt it by remembrance.

But that couldn't be the case. It just couldn't. So she walked into the secluded part of the outside garden that led into the woods, remembering his glare, the glare she could never forget.

She pushed the tree branches out of the way, expecting to see his face. But she was almost shocked when he wasn't there. More so, she was heartbroken. And that completely ruled out everywhere he could possibly have been. It was official: he left the palace.

Vira sighed with a punctured feeling in her heart as she made her way back to the outside and into the palace. She thought feeling alone was bad, but losing someone after she longed to see them again was a feeling she had only felt one other time.

Three more days went by, and Vira hadn't even gotten a note from him. Loneliness pooled up inside of her until it showed. For the first day and a half he was gone, she would walk the halls to ensure she hadn't just missed him. But he hadn't shown. For the rest of the second day and the day following, she only found herself with the energy to sit in her room and stare at the painting as she sipped her tea slowly in anticipation. The painting itself was the only proof that he was real other than the emotional pain.

Vira didn't know how to get over him. She really didn't. She sat there and tried for hours a day until she fell asleep each and every night, dreaming only of him and what happened the night before he left. But even that depressed her even more when she realized it hadn't actually happened.

All of the possibilities circled her mind of what could have happened. He could have been captured by Aleski if he would have gotten out, then hypnotized him not to tell anyone. But as Vira walked the halls, not even Aleski was seen.

Perhaps Cassius snuck out of the palace and was approached by a noble who then killed him. But that made no sense, as no nobles found their way to or around the palace unless asked or invited.

But still, that wouldn't stop Cassius from coming back to the palace to live the life he had been living as an imposter guard for the past several days. Any possibilities of encounters causing him to leave seemed unrealistic, considering that for the three days he was gone, she hadn't heard of him or any vampire encounters. It would have become common knowledge, and possibly made the tabloids as well. She would have known if they killed him. So at least there was still a big possibility that he was still alive somewhere.

It wasn't like Cassius to just leave. At least, in the time Vira had gotten to know him, the crown was important to him, more than anything, and she had hoped he felt similarly about her.

Vira shrieked at the fact that maybe he fled the palace because of her. Maybe their romantic night was real, and no dreams occurred that night other than the one he shook her out of. She knew she saw eyes staring back at her in the dark, so it couldn't have just been her imagination. Perhaps he regretted their intimacy. It was clear that Cassius hated skin to skin contact and valued his personal space. So of course, Vira blamed herself for falling for him. But he made the move on her if what she remembered was real. He soaked her right up. He indulged in her, and he couldn't get enough for her. So she couldn't stop wondering if he had made the mistake of taking her into his arms, and if she had made a mistake falling for the enemy who tried to kill her, then reciprocated the falling.

ISLE TROUBLE

On the third night, the door opened, letting a small amount of light seep into her room. It had woken her up shortly after she had fallen asleep.

The figure was of a man, recognized to be one of the guards. It seemed strange to her at first that a guard would come into her room at night. Perhaps he was here to ask her why Aleski has been gone. Maybe Altha had spread word about them.

The guard turned back to the door to close it carefully to keep quiet.

"Excuse me?" Vira called out.

Whatever his reasoning was wasn't enough to barge into her room late at night to not only wake her up but startle her.

Vira's pulse rose and her hands began to shake.

The man turned back around after locking the door.

"Who are you and what do you want from me?" she asked, attempting to sound threatening.

The guard took off his hat and set it on the ground. Then, he kicked off his boots and set them with his hat.

Whoever the man was seemed like no prowler as slow as he was moving, but he hadn't said a word this far, nor answered any of her questions.

So Vira lit the candle on her bedside table to gain subtle light in the room.

It was in fact no guard, but Cassius.

Vira's heart pounded with shock, relief and utter excitement. She wanted to grab him and pull him on top of her, but he seemed down about something.

The best feeling hit her when she realized the other night wasn't a dream, but instead a night to remember.

"Cassius?" she called out.

He finally looked back up at her and made his way to her bed. He sat on it next to her and sighed as he underwhelmingly said, "Queen, we've got a problem."

"What is it?" Vira sat up in her bed.

"Well, Wintercastle isn't doing too well right now without anyone to rule the isle," he explained.

"Oh." Her voice filled with sorrow. "What does that mean for our plan?"

"Well, it's going to have to move along, but it may move along slower now," he sighed.

Vira didn't know if it joyed her or not to hear. Half of her wanted more than anything to spend more time with him, but the island in trouble was more of an issue than she realized.

"So, when do you have to go back?" Vira asked.

"Actually, that's what I wanted to talk to you about," Cassius replied.

"Because I can get the crown for you while you're gone. I just have to make sure I make all of the right moves," Vira went on.

Cassius paused. It seemed as though he was getting ready to say something. Instead, he pursed his lips and silently laughed. "No, Vira." He shook his head as the laughing smile stuck on his face.

"No?" She cocked her head.

"No, we need to work on you now," he said. "You know, what you're going to get out of this."

"Ah." She shook her head in realization that she had forgotten all about deciding what she was going to get out of helping the soon to be vampire ruler of Wintercastle. "Right."

"Let me guess." He rolled his eyes. "You still don't know what you want from me?"

"I just…" She sighed as she attempted to gather her words. "I've been so busy with everything, it's just slipped past my mind."

"And that's what we're here to figure out now. It's been long enough." Cassius' voice softened when he said, "Besides, you've helped me so much. And for almost no reason at all. It's time for us to focus on you now."

Vira smiled and blushed when she said, "You're right, but Cassius, but how am I supposed to choose if I don't even know what is offered?"

"That's why I was going to ask." He leaned in closer to her, leaning down as he propped his elbow on the pillow. "I'm supposed to make an announcement at Wintercastle tomorrow. In fact, I had almost no time to get here. They've been hounding me and it's been stressful." Vira could tell he was nervous when he ended his sentence with, "Come."

"You want me to come with you to Wintercastle?" Vira didn't know whether to light up or shrivel in anxiousness. She didn't know what to think of it at first. She wondered first how much the isle had gone down in flames since the war. And at that, she wondered if she'd be risking her lives by going to people who wanted her, the ruler of Siciland's step daughter, dead. She was, after all, one of the people who caused the isle's misery.

Cassius nodded. "I've got a few things in mind. It would be better if you saw them in person."

Vira's eyebrows drew together in anticipation, weighing out the good and the bad of going with him back to his isle. "What would I tell my father?"

"Tell him you're going to visit someone. Tell him you're going to explore. You're an adult, aren't you?" he asked.

"Well," Vira sighed. "It doesn't feel that way sometimes. I'm trapped, you see? I can barely move."

"Ah," Cassius nodded. He seemed let down. "Let me know tomorrow, okay?"

"Okay," Vira nodded. "I will."

Really, she needed to think about it. There were too many things to work through and, in terms of time, she had to think fast. It was, after all, yet another mission she'd have to go on aside from the one she had already been voyaging with the crown.

"So, tell me, what's going on exactly at the isle?" Vira asked, supposing that it would help her decide if she knew more about the state Wintercastle was in.

"They don't believe I'm a king until I have something to show for it," he explained.

"The crown." Vira's eyebrows drew together. "Shouldn't they know your uncle was king? You were his nephew and that makes you a prince, doesn't it?"

Cassius nodded his head. "The crown means important things in the isle. Almost everyone fights for it. But only us vampires can claim power."

"Why is it that you vampire's claim power over the land?" Vira asked.

"See, we have the power, some of the vampires who came before me had the gift of mind control that would give them the power to stay on top as the nobles willingly let them take advantage," Cassius explained. "But now that I'm the only one, I can't make that call."

"You can't control minds?" Vira asked.

"No, I was never blessed with that gift." His face filled with doubt.

"Do you have a gift?" She felt like she should have known this by now.

"Maybe." He bobbed his head. "I just haven't had anyone to test it out on yet."

"What would you need to test out?" she asked.

"I'm not going to hurt you." He shook his head. "And I would have to in order to prove my gift to myself."

"Ah," she nodded her head. She felt skimped on the information. "So, what do you *think* your gift might be?"

"I think I have the power to save people," he responded.

"Save people? From what?" she asked.

Cassius hesitated to respond. "You'll see one day if we're meant to be."

Vira couldn't tell if her heart had dropped or mended in a way only done by the truth. Perhaps she would, after all, listen to Altha. But fate seemed like a cop out to her.

She wondered if fate really meant anything, or existed at all. Her and Zereck were clear fate, by many reasons, but perhaps it was just those who had a unique story.

"You really believe we may or may not be meant to be?" Vira almost sounded offended. "Are we really going to let the universe decide that?"

"Vira, I—"

"What if nothing lines up properly, the gods know it already has, but we still end up together because we *want* to?" She finally said what she had been thinking all along.

"Vira, you really think I meant it like that?" He picked up on her unease.

"Fate? What if fate is a joke? What if soulmates are a joke?" she continued her rant. "Cassius, I've never said this before out loud, but…" She walked over to the canvas she had painted and lifted the towel off of it. She brought it closer to him and when he realized what it was, his eyes grew wide. "I never thought there was another way for me. And sometimes I still don't know if I will survive what my life has come to. But one thing I know of is you are the ice to my fire, Cassius, and I'm a fool for you. You calm the monster inside of me who fuels my anger and tells me that I'm never going to belong to anyone. Or that I'm greedy and jealous of someone who has less than me and that I'm a fool for it." Vira looked down at the painting and sighed as she said, "But you make me believe for minutes at a time that killing you was the worst thought to cross my mind."

Cassius sat there in silence, taking in what he had just heard Vira say. The only sound in the entire room was the sound of Vira's heart beating and her breath heavy.

He finally broke the silence when he said, "You think I don't *want* you?" Now it was him who almost sounded offended. "I do." His voice grew louder. "And you are my deepest desire."

"Then what's with fate?" Vira asked.

"I didn't believe in fate. But we are opposites. We are fire and ice, my queen, and if we were not meant to be, we wouldn't be working together here, falling accidentally and perhaps irrevocably." He paused to gather his thoughts. "But how do we know that the worst is yet to come?"

Vira cocked her head at him.

"We will have to separate soon, we just have to. Our time is coming to an end. I'm going back to my island to live my life and you're staying here to live yours." It seemed like he would have cried if he was able to.

"I had no intention of falling, Cassius," Vira said. "This wasn't part of the plan." She set the canvas back on the easel without covering it back up, then sat on her bed next to him and dug her hands in her face.

"Neither did I," he agreed. "I had no plan of surviving either, and if that doesn't mean something already, I don't know what does."

Vira lifted her face from her hands. Everything that had happened this far already seemed not to go to plan. She wondered what else wouldn't go to plan. Perhaps, there was the possibility of everything. Or, perhaps there was the possibility that the rest of the world needed Cassius to survive in order for another war to not break out and overthrow the mortals. Without Cassius, the noble mortals would gain power over Wintercasle as it seemed, and that would open up doors that should have stayed shut.

Vira lifted her head from her hand and noticed Cassius' gaze on her seemed to stick the entire time. This time, he wasn't under stress any longer. Something had changed in his facial expression. His dark eyes glared at her as if saying that his deepest desire was Vira and Vira only.

"Something like this only happens for me once in a solar eclipse," he whispered.

His soft smile rubbed off on Vira, and she soon lightened up. It was as if all of the worries had washed away, and nothing went on in the world but the two of them.

She could feel Cassius subtly lean in slowly, then all at once. He grabbed her face with his cold hands and kissed her lips slowly yet softly.

Give me more than that, Cassius, Vira thought.

So she kissed him harder, and all of her worries melted completely. He leaned her down further to the bed after he moved one of his hands to the back of her head. Vira grabbed his torso, and pulled it on top of her, their bodies closing the gap that was between them. She ran her fingers through his hair, as they moved themselves higher and higher onto the bed. He pressed his palm into the mattress deep as he continued to kiss her, as both of their breaths grew heavier.

He paused as he slowly lifted his face from hers, looking deeply into her eyes. His head bent down to her neck and kissed her neck softly, sending a chill down her spine. He looked back up at her like he was about to say something, then didn't. He seemed interrupted by her beauty.

"I should get some rest," Vira whispered with a smile as she noticed her eyes were heavy. She grabbed his head to kiss him softly one last time as he was still above her, looking down at her.

Cassius nodded, smiling as Vira cozied herself deeper into her bed to fall asleep.

He attempted to roll over to the other side of the bed, but she grabbed him, keeping most of him on top of her.

"Wait, Cassius?" she said, still touching his arm. He looked down at her, smile persisting.

"Yes?" he asked, still somewhat looking at her.

"Can you stay here? You know, until I wake up?" She hesitated to ask.

"Ah, you want me to sleep in bed with you?" He smirked. "Instead of listening to a dozen guys snoring for hours straight until I go insane? Deal." He played it off as if there was another reason he'd rather sleep in Vira's room.

"I just want you here with me," she sighed.

Cassius layed down entirely, letting his head fall to her chest and his arms wrap around the rest of her tighter than he even knew. His hair was soft against Vira's chin, leaving her with a smile as she began to doze off.

It was seconds after Vira's eyes had shut and she nodded off that she felt a chilled peck on her forehead and the ice cold, comforting hand of his as he held her cheek, then whispered, "Anything for you, my queen."

All she could feel then was Cassius returning to the position he was in before, and all had been magical in the moment. Vira could have stayed here forever.

TRUST

Vira's eyes shot open as the morning had come. It had been unnecessary to look over to even search the room to know Cassius had still been by her side, just as he promised.

A gentle touch to her arm told her that. His chilled, soft finger grazed through her hair. Vira wanted to stay here forever, just being with him as he showed her affection she never thought she'd long for.

A small grin stuck on Vira's face as she laid there, enjoying Cassius now that he was back.

"Morning, queen." He must have noticed Vira's eyes were open.

Vira rolled over to look up at him. "How'd the night go?" she asked as she sat up.

"It was great if you ask me." The smile on his face looked like he thought something was funny. "You had quite the dream last night, didn't you?"

"I did?" Vira hadn't even remembered dreaming of anything.

"Well, that's what you're tossing and turning said to me." He bobbed his head.

"Ah," she nodded. "Could be from stress. I do that."

"Ah," he repeated.

A sudden knock on the door startled them both.

"Breakfast is ready," a man's voice said.

It had to have been the servant. He would bring Vira breakfast to her room almost every day.

"Thank you," she said, looking at Cassius like she was saying *get out of sight*.

Vira opened the door right after Cassius quickly took his guard hat and boots and hid under her bed with them.

"Here you are." He handed her a tray with a waffle on it and a side of oranges with a cup of tea to drink.

"Thank you." Vira took the plate and nodded one time to him.

The servant left right after and Vira closed the door. She turned back to her bed and walked towards it.

"After breakfast is done, we better get on with the day," Vira suggested.

Cassius appeared once again.

She sat on her bed and continued, "We wouldn't want anyone onto us any more than they already are."

Cassius' eyes grew wide. He sat on her bed and said, concerned, "Already are?"

"I didn't tell you?" Vira smacked her palm to her forehead. Perhaps she was too busy last night with Cassius. "Altha thinks I'm in a relationship with one of the guards." She pointed to the name tag and said, "Aleski."

"What?" He froze.

"Yeah, it slipped my mind." She forked some of the waffle into her mouth. "Oh, and one of the other guards told me you're rather quiet lately. More so that Aleski usually is."

"Has this rumor gotten around to everyone, you know, that you're with a guard?" It was clear that he was apprehensive to hear the answer even though he asked the question.

Vira shook her head. "Not that I know of." She held her hand in front of her waffle chewing mouth as she said, "If Altha does what I ask."

"I'm staying away from most people because of my cold. Go with that," he said.

"I got it." Vira nodded, then lifted her tea cup up to her mouth to sip on it.

She looked over at him as she observed him sitting calmly as she finished off her tea.

"So, what's it like not to eat anything?" Getting to know Cassius as a vampire grew her fascination.

"I'm only ever hungry for the one thing I can't have. Imagine that, I suppose," he explained.

"So you're starving?" She raised an eyebrow.

"I'm able to contain it after many many years of practice." He seemed proud to say that.

He *looked* like he had been a vampire for some time. Perhaps it was his containment in general at first, and how he didn't eat Aleski that made her assume so from the start. He was also seemingly older than her. In vampire years, he's in his mid to late twenties. That differed from Vira, who was in her early twenties.

"How long have you been a vampire?" She felt like she had to know.

Cassius looked to think back through decades of time. "It's too hard to remember, but I was twenty five when they found me, and twenty seven when they changed me." That would bring him to twenty seven now.

"Changed you?" Vira asked.

"Well, I was trying to find my way here, Siciland, to live a better life, and because I heard the best healers were here. I thought for sure they'd be able to fix my deadly medical condition. There's a lot of poverty in Wintercastle if you're not royalty," he explained.

But Vira realized it hadn't seemed as far off from Siciland as he thought.

"But one of the spies who wanted to catch me crossing the borders attacked me, and I was brought back," he continued.

"Spies? You mean…" Vira knew.

"A werewolf."

Vira's eyes grew wide as she asked, "How are you not dead?" But she realized technically he was, even if that wasn't the point.

"The king came to save me from their kind, but there was no need." He smiled. "I won."

Vira's face switched to a look of disbelief.

"You're amazing, then," she praised him. "Perhaps it's best for Siciland that I flew you back to your country or else we would have been defeated by you alone."

Cassius laughed. "I know you're exaggerating." He shook his head. "But I took the Alpha's mate."

Vira's eyes grew even wider. She thought back to the war and how she never saw the Alpha wolf with a wife, or anyone to love by his side other than his descendants, one of which being Altha's shifter mate Zereck.

"Do you think they remember you?" Vira's voice shook.

"You tend to change your appearance slightly when you turn cold." Cassius shook his head. "But my only answer to that is I'd hope not."

"Wow." Vira was taken aback. "You killed my best friend's boyfriend's mother."

"She tried to kill *me*," he said in defense.

"I get it, that's why I almost killed you," she resonated. "But how did you become a vampire?"

"I had no dad to serve me at the time, which is why I was deep and desperate in poverty," he explained. "He and the wolf shifters went way back. They always thought we were innocent little mortals. But I proved them wrong that day, which is why I was crowned a prince alongside his son who later became like a cousin to me, Rory. That made the king like an uncle to me. After that, they asked me if I'd like to live forever as a vampire in exchange to rise out of my poverty, which I was in no position to pass up."

"You became a vampire all to rise out of poverty?" Vira's voice raised in pitch.

"It may seem taboo to you, step daughter of the island's ruler," he joked. "But it was more than that. It would give me the freedom of no longer needing to worry about dying, which seemed soon to come at the time."

"You make me feel privileged," she responded.

"I make you recognize your privilege, more so," he corrected her.

Vira laughed, then paused to listen to the banter that went on right outside of her door. The hallways were filling up already with people in the place, which meant her and Cassius would have to be on their way soon.

"We better get going. People are already starting to fill the halls," Vira suggested as she dropped the fork back onto the near empty plate and sat it aside.

By the time she looked over, Cassius was already putting his guard uniform back on after taking his mask from the hat and securing it back on his face.

"Let me know today." Cassius winked. "I'd like you to come with me."

Vira nodded, huffing a breath of anxiousness. "Sure thing, I'll let you know."

She didn't think before she opened the door, as she always does and had become muscle memory to her at that point.

"See you later, Queen Vira," he joked as he looked outside the opened door, then his eyes grew wide.

The door opened, and there stood Altha in conversation with one of the guards. Suddenly, everyone's eyes looked the same.

Altha's mouth hung open and if the guard was not dressed as covered, so would he.

"I knew it!" the guard yelled.

Altha pretended to be shocked, as Vira could only tell.

Cassius fled the room and darted down the hallway, acting somewhat natural, like he was just trying to get on with his job.

"He had to get to work," Vira answered for him.

"You mean to tell me you're having an affair with Aleski?" The guard was taken aback. He said affair as if it was a sin to fall in love.

"No, no affair, we're just…" Vira gulped, unsure of what to say.

It did look sketchy that Cassius, all of a sudden, came out from Vira's bedroom first thing in the morning.

"Just what? In love?" he badgered her. "The man is ten years older than you. Your father would never approve."

"I'm an adult." Vira crossed her arms and stood up straighter.

"You're the *princess*. It's different," he argued.

Vira switched her gaze to Altha, wondering why she was talking to the guard. She still had a look on her face of shock, but Vira still had yet to know why.

"Altha." Vira bobbed her head into her room. "I'd like to talk, please?"

Altha nodded, then walked into Vira's room with her head hung low like she was embarrassed.

"Please don't let it get back to my father, I'd like to be the one to tell him," she pleaded. "And we're not ready yet," was all she could think to say.

It seemed as though each day that went by made things worse for her. Although, she had also found it a surprise how long it had taken to catch onto both her and Cassius. At least, he was of no knowledge to anyone except Vira by now.

The guard man sighed, then rolled his eyes as he went back to walking the halls.

Vira turned around and closed the door behind her.

"Altha, what happened?" She held her hands up in the air like Altha had done something.

Altha sighed. "The guard approached me, asking if I knew what was going on with you. He said he knew I was closest to you out of everyone in the palace," she explained. "Well, I panicked and told him I wasn't sure of anything."

"So you didn't tell him anything?" Vira's eyebrows drew together.

Altha shook her head. "It wasn't until you and him walked out that he suspected anything at all between you and the guard."

"They've been onto Aleski, claiming that he's quieter now. I knew that," Vira explained. "But you knew about Aleski and I. I know because I told you."

"I do remember, but I assumed it would never be my place to tell," she responded.

"Good." Vira nodded once.

Just as Vira was about to ask Altha why she had shown shock, Altha's eyes explored around the room.

"Wow, I would have loved something like this when I was younger. This entire room is twice the size of my dome house now." She was taken aback.

But Vira's eye went right to the painting that she had forgotten to cover up from when she showed Cassius the night prior. Something felt like it dropped in her stomach. Perhaps it was her heart.

"Hey, I didn't know you took up painting." Altha walked over to the painting before Vira could get to it to cover it up.

But the cat was already out of the bag and the damage had already been done. Vira gripped the sides of her hair, nearly yanking it all out. She hated herself for being careless.

"Hey, wait." Vira's face went pale, almost as pale as Cassius'.

For a moment, Vira felt like she could vomit any second.

Altha hadn't said a word as she squinted her eyes at the painting, seeming like she was attempting to put something together, even if she didn't seem to know what.

Vira approached Altha, attempting to shield her away even if it was too late. She had already seen the painting and knew something had to be up.

"I've never seen Aleski," Altha turned to Vira and said, "But I would have never imagined him to look like this under his uniform."

"Yeah, it's a funny world." Vira nervously laughed.

"No, really, he still looks familiar to me." She nodded her head in observation with her pointer finger on her chin.

"Well, I don't know, Al." Vira's voice shook.

Altha stared deep into Vira's eyes, giving her a look of suspicion. "I know that can't be Aleski."

"How do you know?" Vira got defensive. "You've never seen him without his uniform on."

"You," Altha balled up her fists, "aren't telling me the truth? I thought I was the one you trusted."

"Look, Altha, you're my friend. My best friend. But this, I cannot tell you and I'm sorry." Vira sighed as she turned away not to face Altha.

"Why can't you tell me?" Altha came around to face Vira again.

But Vira's head still looked to the floor in sorrow. Her chest started to feel blue again, like her time with Cassius was diminished, more so, ruined.

A small tear drop fell down her cheek as she remained silent.

Altha's mouth hung open in shock. "This isn't Aleski, is it?"

But still, Vira's stomach felt like it had been punched and if she spoke, tears would come bursting down her face.

It was clear Altha had about a thousand questions, but she seemed to only focus on Vira and getting the words out of her.

"You're in a secret relationship with someone even more forbidden than Aleski, aren't you?" Altha concluded. "But you're going to tell me who it is."

"I said I couldn't." Vira finally managed to speak some words.

"I fell in love with a wolf shifter, Vira, back when it wasn't even allowed. They were after me. They all wanted to kill me. Whatever you've done with this man couldn't be any worse than what I've done."

Vira sniffled as she looked up. She sat on her bed and exhaled, wiping the tears away.

She took a deep breath before saying, "I'm in love with a vampire."

And just like that, Altha's eyes grew wide. She glanced over at the painting in realization of where she had remembered him from.

Vira wondered just how much she trusted Altha. She pondered in the moment of shocking silence whether she should tell her about how Cassius, who was nearly her vampire mate, killed the Alpha's wife, who was Altha's wolf shifter mate's own mother.

"He ran towards you during the war." Altha was finally able to speak again after processing what she had heard. "I remember, because I was the one who alerted you he was running your way. We both watched him fly across the sky, farther than we could even see."

"He ended up back at his isle. I saved his life." Vira shook her head as if she regretted it, even though by now, she knew it was her biggest non-regret.

"He's alive?" Altha asked a little too loud.

"Well," Vira joked. "He's here and I'm helping him find the vampire king's crown in order for him to go back to Wintercastle and leave us alone forever."

"You're helping him find the dead king's crown? Why?"

Vira nodded. "He said he'd give me something in return."

"Like what?" Altha made her way to the bed to sit next to Vira in concern.

"I don't know yet. That's the one flaw to our plan," she said, even though there seemed to be many more. "He wants me to come with him to Wintercastle Palace

206

tomorrow with some items in mind he proposes I'd like in return."

"Are you going?" Altha asked.

"I'd like to, but I'm a princess. I don't mean to minimize my privilege or sound problematic, but I'm locked up. How will I ever come up with an excuse to leave the palace for a day or two?"

Altha sat in anticipation for seconds before saying, "You're going." She sounded like she meant it, too.

"What?" Vira asked.

"You're going," Altha repeated. "I'll request to Sir Arthur myself that we need help building Zereck and I's new house, and you'd like to grant us the favor."

Vira's face lit up. The idea had gone over her head before, but she was lucky Altha was smart enough to come up with one and have a good enough friend to go along with it.

"You'd do that for me?" Vira smiled.

"I'd do anything for true love," she responded.

"I..." Vira sighed, unable to string the words together. "I'm worried that he and I are true loves who will never be able to be together. Our fate be damned."

"I thought the same thing of Zereck." Altha shrugged.

"But the entire island pretty much will be against me if they know." Vira shook as she said, "I might die if they found out I let a vampire roam the halls of this precious palace for days on end, much less than fell in love with him."

"You really love him, don't you?" Altha glanced back at the painting again.

Vira nodded, too apprehensive to even say it out loud.

"Love will find its way, like I told you," Altha assured her.

After a moment of anticipation, Vira concluded the conversation by saying, "I better let Cassius know that I'm going with him tomorrow. He'll be excited to hear the good news."

And so was Vira. It was an alluring thought to know she'd spend time with him without feeling like she had to walk on eggshells to do so.

She opened the door back up again and looked back at Altha who was approaching to walk out the door. "Thank you," she said.

"Of course, and to be clear, I don't need anything in return," Altha joked.

ATTACHMENT

One thing Vira did happen to know without needing to find out was the fact people were now definitely talking about her and Aleski.

She could feel it every time she had gotten to walk the halls. By the time he would come back to the palace after his memory being wiped, she knew she and Cassius would have to put on a fake show, addressing their fake break up.

Nearly the only person Vira still had trust left for was Altha. She could have decided to hate Cassius. And she had every right to. They viewed vampires as killers, even if they didn't know they were vampires at the time.

But now, Vira knew she needed to find Cassius fast. Perhaps they'd need to leave today, and now wait for more to happen before their plans diminish.

So she headed towards the hallway, aiming her way to the back of the palace. The halls were bare compared to the amount of people who were around within the last couple of days Cassius wasn't around.

At one point, Vira's step father caught her eye. He was in conversation with Altha already. The two must have crossed paths, and Altha must have already been asking him about Vira's plans to help out with building their house.

As she walked closer to them unavoidably, her step father's gaze switched to her once he noticed her in the hallway.

"Ah, my darling," he called out.

Vira didn't say anything as they made their way to each other. She was too busy trying to contain herself from the guilt.

"You're going to the healer's house to help them? How thoughtful." He smiled.

"Oh, yeah, I'm always glad to help," she lied.

"Just don't dirty your dress is my one command," he insisted.

"Got it," Vira underwhelmingly nodded. "I'll be home in less than a few days."

Vira concluded their conversation when she walked past him as he smiled. On the inside, she had blushed, and the excitement built up inside of her. It was now that she realized she wanted to go with Cassius, even if she had things to be worried about when she went. It almost seems surreal that her step father would have agreed to let Vira escape the palace for any reason.

Now, she was excited to share the news with him.

Once she neared the back side of the palace, there were too many people walking around for her comfort zone.

She wanted to try and find Cassius, but there was no use. She had hoped it hadn't gotten to her step father at this point, and it didn't seem to yet, thankfully. So being seen with Cassius would have made matters worse.

Instead, she made her way to the meditation room. She figured since she'd be at Wintercastle Palace before the day is over, it would be in her benefit to work on keeping her magic under control. It would be a shame if her power would give her away, or if she'd accidentally destroy something while she was there.

The snake was silent that day. Perhaps it was a sign. An urban legend said if the Kharmat was quiet, it would bring good luck or meant something good would come the person's way.

Soft music played in the background as Vira positioned herself on the mat. She closed her eyes and took a deep breath in, letting it out as she crossed her legs together.

This time, she only felt it necessary to sit and think. Sometimes, all she needed was a safe, quiet space. This room had been a bonus with the floral aroma and the extra dim lights.

But Vira should have known better from the last time she had been here. Her mind raced, a lot. But her worries weren't enough to overpower the good. She was about to leave, and for once and for all.

What she pondered the most was when Cassius mentioned to Vira about not growing attached to her. She wondered if it was beginning to be a fear of hers, too. Perhaps going to his palace will only strengthen her connection to him even if they don't mean it. The thought of being attached to him scared her, causing her forehead to tense. He was becoming enjoyable company. Everything seemed to happen too sudden. It snuck up on her. She realized now that Altha asked her if she loved Cassius and she nodded, meaning it was too late to stop the attachment. It pained her to know it would come to a violent end, having to hide her misery from everyone when he left, and she would never see him again.

But Vira now wondered another thing, yet another question she demanded to know. Had Cassius grown attached to her as well?

18

SNEAKING OUT

I t seemed like it was all day that Vira waited for the moment that darkness came. She felt like a teenager sneaking out to meet a guy. She felt rebellious for the first time. After all, this *was* the most she had ever gone against her step father. Jitters filled her body, but they faded away once he arrived.

Cassius opened the door to her room.

"So?" he asked.

Vira nodded and said, "I'd like to go." She smiled and stood up, walking closer to him with a smile.

"You figured everything out that quick?" Cassius sounded confused.

"I did, and I'm ready. For real." Her nerves were wild when she first thought of the negatives of the trip but now, it only excited her. "Altha told my father I'll be helping her and Zereck build their house."

Cassius nodded in approval. "Wow, you really did take care of things."

"I'd like to leave before the sun rises," Vira said as she walked over to her closet to open it. "I don't need anyone seeing either of us and I'm not sure I want to see what happens to you when vitamin D hits your bare skin."

Cassius' eyes were glued to her as she took a smaller dress from the hanger.

"You took the words right out of my mouth." He stared at her with desire again, just like he had the other night at the garden. It was those looks that urged her to know the truth about him, the answer to the questions she pondered at the meditation room.

"Meanwhile," Vira kept talking as she walked into the bathroom and flicked the light on, then moved far enough into it for him not to see her change. She wasn't ready for that yet. "I'd like to hear about what *happens* when your skin touches sunlight," she yelled from the bathroom so he could hear her loud and clear.

The dress she now had on after slipping it over her head once she had taken the other dress off had spaghetti straps. It was styled more delicately, more of an underdress. But it was lightweight, and built for traveling far by foot and long distances.

"I'm not so sure I want you to see that," he said.

When Vira came out of the bathroom, she folded her arms at him. "I asked you to tell, not show."

"We should probably get ready for when we leave. How are we going to do this?" He was clearly trying to change the subject.

"Well, I think you will keep your guard uniform on up until we exit the premises," Vira explained.

"We will have to go back to the war site. That way we'll have a boat to get there," he suggested.

It came to Vira's attention that if she was Cassius, she wouldn't have been able to handle going back to the battleground where all of his family members were decapitated.

"Are you sure you're okay with that?" she asked just to make sure.

She couldn't tell if Cassius was worried or not, the way he stood completely still and his voice sounded underwhelmed as always.

"Don't worry about it. Main point here is we need to go to the palace." He shook his head.

"But it's for my sake, right? I wouldn't want you to go through all this trouble just so I could decide what I'd like out of this. If it's any consolation, I can pick something out in my head right now if you'd prefer."

Cassius shook his head again while she was talking. "I must be there for more than your sake, but the isle's. This night as we travel there, we may ponder the possibilities of your gift, but when the morning comes, I must make an announcement. The nobles will all gather around the palace front, waiting for me to come out on the platform to speak."

"Oh," Vira exhaled. "This speech, what are you going to say?"

"I must only inform them that everything is moving along as planned, and that with a slow rebuild, our monarchy system will be back up and functioning as normal. They're like children who need to hold their mother's hand to know they're safe in terms of these announcements," he explained.

"And what will I be doing?" Vira asked.

"You will stand back. They don't need to know that you're with me at the palace." He stepped closer to her.

Vira sat on the bed. "It's getting late."

"The halls are silent now," he observed.

Vira got up from her bed and peered through the peephole.

"I don't see anyone nearby," she said.

"Tell me when the coast is clear," Cassius said as he approached the door. "And meet me at the back door. I'll be waiting for you in the woods."

Vira nodded with a smile. She opened the door and poked her head out. She looked both ways down the halls and both were vacant.

She glanced back at Cassius and whispered, "You're clear."

He zipped past Vira impossibly fast no more than a second after, nearly startling her.

Before leaving her bedroom, she grabbed a tote that hung on the side of her vanity.

When she stepped into the hallway, she closed the door to her room silently, then crept the halls as she made her way to the back door.

FROZEN HEART

I t was a sensation of relief when Vira made it out the back door without getting caught. It wasn't abnormal for her to be near the back door, but the fact that it was late at night would alarm anyone who saw her.

She made her way into the woods that Cassius and her had found themselves many times before: the secluded garden.

He turned around once she approached.

"Are you ready to do this, Queen Vira?" he asked.

Vira nodded, letting out an exhale to calm herself of the anxiety that came with knowing that what she was doing was wrong.

"I guess so," she replied.

"Alright." Cassius bobbed his head and began walking further into the forest.

Vira was several steps behind him, but tried her best to catch up to him.

Cassius stopped and looked behind himself at her and said, "You coming or what?" jokingly.

"I am, you're just faster than me, I guess," she said as she looked down at her shoes, which were heels, the only shoes she was even allowed to own.

On second thought, Vira didn't know if she'd be able to make it all the way to Wintercastle Isle in mini heels on foot. The forest was a bit muddy as if it had rained previously.

But still she kept walking.

The heel on her shoe sunk into a soft spot on the ground. She gasped, causing Cassius to look back.

He sighed, then said, "Obviously this isn't going to work."

Vira looked up after lifting her shoe out of the ground. It nearly slid off her foot as she did, and it was now covered in mud.

"You might be right," she agreed.

"Looks like we're going to have to do this differently." He walked toward her as he spoke.

"Differently?" She cocked her head.

He stood inches away from her and nodded with a slight smile. Without a word, he wrapped his chilled arms around her waist and picked her up bridal style.

"Uh, Cassius, are you sure you'd want to—" she tried to ask, doubting that he would be able to carry her the entire way.

"Hold on tight," he interrupted, giving her butterflies.

Without another thought, Vira wrapped her arms, clasping them behind his neck. She was still confused about what he meant by *another way.*

But it wasn't long until she found out. Right after, he took off running abnormally fast. Faster than any mortal or sorcerer would be able to. Vira flinched startled, gripping him tighter from the thrill of moving too fast as the gust of wind hit her in the face simply from the movement.

She kept her eyes closed for the majority of the time. The only scarce times she opened her eyes were only to note how far they had gone. The moon shone onto both of them, being the only source of lighting. But even that was mostly covered by clouds. It was romantic, even more romantic than the dimness of the palace.

Vira wondered if Cassius would need to catch his breath anytime soon. Just watching him move as fast as he did made her want to catch hers. But then she remembered he was a vampire, and they never needed to.

Soon, she felt herself come to halt.

"You're going to be dizzy if I set you down right away," he spoke into her ear.

Vira opened her eyes, seeing that she was already to the battleground where one of the boats was still floating far out along the shoreline.

The dizziness hit her not long after she took in her surroundings. Her head spun as she held it and she closed her eyes again, laying her head on Cassius' strong chest.

"I told you," he said.

Once her vision went clear again and she was able to catch her spinning head, she lifted her head to look up at Cassius.

"We must go," she said. "We have some important things to do before we need to come back here."

Cassius nodded, then set her down.

Vira watched him as he peered out into the moonlit ocean gleaming upon the steadily moving water.

The small boat was too far out into the ocean to be able to reach. Cassius stepped back without looking, fixated on the boat. It seemed as though he was scared of the water, like he was allergic to it. His eyes squinted at the boat as he ran fast, then jumped, reminiscent of the war when Vira had struck him.

He landed on his feet into the boat and held onto the sides of it when water splashed up onto the sides. It looked even smaller now Cassius was inside of it. Vira wondered if there would even be enough room to fit her inside of it as well.

He took an oar that was still inside the boat and made his way to the shoreline up to Vira.

"It looks like only this small life boat was left from the war. It must have been too far for them to get to it and destroy it," he said once he was close enough to her.

Vira nodded, then looked down at his hand as he held it out to her. She took it, surprised he cared to help her get into the boat. Another thing that surprised her was how he seemed to want her specifically to be in front of him in the boat.

"The nose of it is smaller, better fit for someone like you." He smirked.

Vira rolled her eyes as she looked back at him, stepping her way into the boat and releasing his hand.

She felt him sit down behind her as she fixed her dress neatly after sitting down. The boat was, indeed, small enough to only hold the two of them with no extra room to spare. His knees squeezed the sides of her tightly in an attempt to fit himself all the way in the boat. His legs extended out to the sides of her, creating an even distribution throughout the entire space.

Cassius began paddling the boat out deeper into the ocean. He didn't speak a word until he seemed to get the hang of rowing the boat in the direction of where they were headed, which seemed south west of where they were near Davelburn and Maycaster.

"So, have you ever been to Wintercastle?" Cassius was obviously just attempting to make conversation.

Vira laughed. "No."

"So, what exactly is it like being a vampire?" Vira asked.

Cassius paused in anticipation before answering. "Well, it's like staying alive when you know you should be dead."

"You think you should be dead?" Vira almost turned all the way around, but the boat moving to the side startled her, thinking that she'd tip it, so she turned back around to let her racing heart settle.

"I think a lot about that sometimes. Just lately, not as much," he replied.

Vira couldn't turn around to see the facial expression on his face, but she had guessed by the tone of his voice it was a grin. But it seemed ironic that he would answer that way, especially considering he was alone and hated by everyone but Vira now.

Vira would have asked why now all of a sudden he hadn't wished he were dead, but his next sentence threw her off.

"I never saw my monarchical blended family care much for me," he went on. Vira's eyes widened at the fact that she had never sympathized with anyone more.

"Was there a vampire princess?" she asked.

"Yes." His voice sounded joyful. "Tons of them."

"And you weren't blood related to any of them?" she asked, no pun intended.

"No."

"Were any of them…" She struggled to find the words to ask what she wanted to ask. "The one?"

Cassius laughed subtly before repeating, "No."

"Were any of them pretty?" She wanted to know his history with other women and if she was the only one.

"Yes. They were all pretty," he responded.

"Did you," Viira took a deep breath before finishing her sentence, "kiss any of them?"

"No," he said sternly. "They were all pretty. But as much as I got to know them, it was like they only wanted to mate."

"And you didn't want that?" she asked, surprised.

"I told you how it is for us the first night I spent in your room. And at that, a lot of the vampire girls wanted someone for that purpose, to be way too intimate with," he explained. "In other words, they had pretty faces. But they weren't beautiful."

Vira grew an ear to ear grin at his words and a rush of serotonin filled up inside of her. Cassius hadn't kissed anyone else, and that drove her wild. In fact, now she knew he waited decades to kiss Vira because she was beautiful to him whether he cared to directly admit it or not.

"What about you, miss flames?" he said sarcastically.

"Huh?" she said as her thoughts were interrupted by him.

"You've been quiet about your life. What's your past like?" he asked.

Vira had to think back to what her life was like before becoming a sorcerer. Nothing intimate came of it with any of the young men she knew. Only thoughts of loneliness and self hatred came to mind.

"My father left me when I was younger. Very young. My mother married the ruler. Half because she said she loved him and half to be able to feed me, clothe and shelter me all at once," Vira explained, for once not hurting on the inside as she spoke about it. "Shortly after, my mother wrapped up her last circus performance as a flamethrower, which ended in a fire accident. All I remembered was some man took me away after covering up my eyes and took me back to my step father."

"And now you're the sorcerer of flames?" he asked, confused.

"They said since I have the heritage of my mother being good with fire, that would be my calling as well." Vira shook her head and looked down. "But I'm not so sure it is anymore. Perhaps they shouldn't have assumed it," she said as if she ever thought it was supposed to be her calling. "Sense then, I've felt too misplaced to even feel like I could be loved. I'm sure many of the guards would have taken their chances on me, but I've always been too closed off for anyone. I won't even hold a conversation for a solid minute."

"You're holding a conversation now," he observed.

Vira's face slightly smiled as she said, "Yeah, I guess I am."

A small sliver of the isle was now visible to the naked eye as Vira squinted her eyes at it. It didn't look much different from Siciland even from a distance, which took vira by surprise. The closer they had gotten to the isle, the more she dreaded the boat ride coming to the end.

The closer they had got to it, the more Vira's mind also wondered what more there was to ask him. Perhaps she still hadn't perfected her conversation skills, regardless of what he said.

"What's it like to be cold?" she asked, nearly face palming herself out of embarrassment for asking such a silly question.

"What's it like being hot?" he asked, causing Vira to warm up.

Vira couldn't help but blush, but was glad she had no choice to turn around so he could see.

"I don't feel it." She shook her head. "It's a weird thought that fire radiates through my veins, yet I don't feel a thing, other than when I'm about to shoot a flame or when I've overheated myself."

"Well then there you go," he said, sounding focused on rowing the boat. "I don't have much to offer you. That's why I told you I didn't want to grow attached to you in the first place the other night."

"What don't you have to offer?" Vira asked.

"Just that what you mentioned. I don't have a beating heart, Vira. I'm stone cold. You don't make my pulse rise, like you might do to other guys. I don't get butterflies in my stomach when I think of you. I wouldn't even be able to cry if you left me. I just wouldn't be able to let it out properly. I'd do something malicious instead."

"Malicious?" Vira's heart skipped a beat when she heard the word.

"Not to you. To someone else to take it out on. Maybe the nosy guard or someone else. Or a wolf," he explained.

Half of Vira wanted to cry, and the other half was confused. If he didn't get the jitters thinking about her, then why would he kiss her, or accidentally call her beautiful, or anything he's said or done to her thus far?

"None of the other men raise my pulse. They don't make my heart flutter, and they don't make me blush at the thought of them. I don't long for their touch or wish to be pressed against them each and every night while I lay awake thinking of them." Vira took a breath before continuing. "I don't understand you sometimes, Cassius." And it was an understatement. It was also long overdue.

"I don't understand me either. I understand if I made you upset." His voice went low.

"I mean seriously," she knew it was time to address the elephant, "you *kissed* me. You wouldn't even kiss the princesses of your kind but you kissed me."

"I know, I—" he started.

Vira's voice rosein offense when she interrupted, "And all this time, I've been paying attention to the way you look at me when you don't think I'd turn back, but I catch you. You know that. And I know you're looking at me with desire, and not the type of desire you get when you're hungry," she ranted. "Why?"

"I'm a stone cold demon. Everyone knows that. I'm not supposed to have emotions or have a soul," he said as he pulled into the shoreline of Wintercastle Isle.

Vira sighed as she gathered her thoughts.

He anchored the boat into the bright sandy dirt with the oar, and then stepped out in front of the boat onto the land.

He held his hand out to Vira and she grabbed it, but looked up at him with suspicious eyes.

"Cassius, I—" she started to say as he pulled her up from the boat and helped her step onto the land.

"Hold that thought," he interrupted as he picked her up again and took off into the direction of the palace Vira could only see from a distance where they were. It wouldn't be able to be missed, as it overlooked the entire isle with it's enormity.

WINTERCASTLE PALACE

The dizziness caught up to Vira as soon as they stopped in front of the palace. The pale gray exterior glistened in the moonlight, similar to Siciland Palace. But that was all Vira was able to tell while her head was still going around.

"Here we are, Wintercastle Palace," he announced as he put her down.

Vira's head slowed down as she rubbed her eyes, then looked up to admire the building. It was a combination mostly of lighter grays and darker grays, not in between, but the detail complimented the colors evenly.

"Wow." She was taken aback as her eyes finally adjusted. "It's beautiful."

"I guess so." Cassius shrugged it off.

He approached the entrance, leaving Vira to follow behind him. The door lifted up. As it did, it hadn't squeaked nor squealed like the palace back where Vira lived, which surprised her, considering this palace had more of a chance of being medieval than the one in Siciland just by the way vampires once lived here.

After the door lifted up, the most beautiful yet dimmed blue theme painted the palace's insides. The silver and blue detail was more eventful in comparison.

"I'd like to show you a few things, if you're up for it," Cassius stepped all the way inside the palace and said.

Vira followed him, her eyes catching more of the detail than before.

"Where are we headed?" Vira finally asked when she snapped out of taking in the palace's beauty.

"Well, let's just say I've had a few things in mind for you. I've thought about it on the boat ride here, and I think at least one of these ought to be a winner," he explained, sounding sure of himself.

"Ah." Vira noticed he didn't entirely answer her question, but perhaps it was better that she was in for a surprise.

The farther down the hallways they walked, the dimmer the lights had gotten. Perhaps Cassius forgot that Vira wasn't a vampire nor had the same super vision vampires had. Compared to the palace she had lived in, she would consider this one near dark, with only small off white light bulbs at every few feet on the walls.

"You like jewelry, don't you?" he asked.

Vira bit her lip. He obviously hadn't gotten to know her as well as she thought he did.

"Yes, sure," she lied, but it was quite obvious in her tone.

It would be a shame if she had gone through all this trouble just for a piece of jewelry, when jewelry already underwhelmed her with having to wear it uncomfortably every day in the first place. But she had hope that there were other things he had to offer with the way it sounded like he had multiple objects in mind.

Cassius stopped at a door and opened it. By the looks of it, Vira could already tell it had to be someone's room by the way hats and long scarfs were hung from the walls.

He held the door, stepping aside for Vira to enter the room. As she did, she knew it definitely had to be someone's room. It was larger than Vira's by a bit.

"This was Queen Charlotte's room," he announced, breaking the silence between them.

"I knew it had to be someone's room," she answered.

She stood back as she watched him maneuver his way around the room like he was searching for something.

He stopped at a large wooden box. He opened it carefully, then turned his head towards Vira, motioning to tell her to come his way.

Once she was near him, she could see exactly why he brought her here in the first place. The queen's jewelry would always be the fanciest and most valuable.

He stood next to her, watching her look through the queen's jewelry. It felt unnatural for Vira, considering she grew up to know it was a sin to root through the queen's belongings. But the only time she had thus far was when there was a reason. This time should slide as well, assuming that because she was helping Cassius, the Queen's supposably nephew, she wouldn't have minded.

"See anything you like?" Cassius asked.

Vira paused, then turned to him with her hand still midway into the jewelry holder. It was all beautiful. The amount of diamonds were fascinating to Vira and the way everything seemed to have a luminescent bluish glow was different, catching Vira's attention. But she still didn't know that the jewelry was worthy of all that she had done.

"Don't you think I should see what else there is to offer first?" she asked.

Really, jewelry hadn't been her thing. And still, she stuck with that, even though she was taken aback by its beauty.

Cassius didn't say anything immediately. Instead, he reached into the holder and took out an amulet style necklace that glistened of white sparkles that hinted at a light blue tone.

He unclasped it and walked behind her. Vira stood still as he wrapped the amulet around her neck and brought the gem part to the front before clasping it into place. Vira fixed her hair as he came back around to the front of her.

"There, in case you change your mind." He smiled when he saw the way it looked on her.

Vira knew the chances were low that she'd change her mind and come back to the Queen's room for jewelry, but she got the chills for more reasons than one when he put the necklace on her.

She followed him out of the room and noticed him looking around, deciding where he wanted to go next.

He looked back at her and said, "You like flowers, don't you?"

They seemed to be headed to a hallway similar in path to the hallway in the castle they would go to a secluded garden.

"I do," she answered. She felt better about the next destination than their last.

He didn't say a word after that. He only guided her wherever he wanted to take her. The halls weren't as dim leading to their next destination, which was better for Vira. If she had squinted her eyes any more than she already had, it would give her a headache.

They turned into a more narrow hallway that led to a door. It was larger than the other ones, but smaller than the front door of the palace.

It was a good thing she admired flower gardens, like the one back at the palace. At least more than jewelry. Even if she almost accidently burnt Altha's sorcery flowers, she still found peace when she stood around them.

But it seemed foolish of Cassius to give her none other than a flower in exchange for helping him find her king's crown, allowing him to crown himself. It was almost an insult to princesses that that would be all they needed to be happy.

"What's out there?" she asked before he opened the door.

"You'll see," he said as he put his hand on the knob and looked back at her. He seemed to never answer her questions at this point, which she grew tired of.

The annoyance came to a halt when he twisted the doorknob and let the door fall open. The moonlight gleamed down perfectly on what looked to be a field of light blue flowers.

Cassius stepped outside, then stopped as Vira came to his side. She was in shock at how beautiful the field was, how the misty glow sprayed off the flowers. It may have been even more beautiful than the garden at the palace Vira lives in.

Vira widened her eyes at the flowers as she came towards them, realizing that they were roses. Small drops of water dropped from the petals and the moist look to them somehow made them even more alluring. She had never seen anything like it before. It still wasn't enough for her, but her eyes were glued to the scene, so she didn't care that it was only flowers she was looking at.

"They're beautiful." She sounded like she meant it.

"We would call them ice roses," he mentioned.

Rightfully so, with the way the ice blue color glistened even when it was mostly dark.

"What do you do here?" she asked.

"Well," he started walking on a bricked path, taking her gently by the arm. She hadn't even noticed until she felt his cold touch on her arm. "We do exactly what you do in your garden. Admire them as we let our minds wander."

"They're beautiful," she said again, still in awe.

"You already said that." Cassius laughed.

Vira shook herself out of the trance. "Oh, I guess I did."

She noticed he still hadn't let go of her arm. But Vira didn't mind it. She was lucky to even get skin contact from him in the first place. But it was no longer a grip. He was only gently touching her at that point.

"You, uh…" Vira cleared her throat. "Cut me off earlier," she mentioned.

"Oh yeah, I did." He laughed.

"So, speaking of ice, you also confuse me," she looked up at him and said.

It was then that his eyebrows drew together and he let his arm drop down to his side.

"How is it that I confuse you?" he asked.

"You say you're ice cold," she went on.

"Uh huh." He nodded his head. "I am. You've touched me before."

"But it's more than just touch," she added. "You say it's your soul, too."

"Yeah." It seemed that he kept his answers short for a reason.

Really, Vira demanded to know how he really felt about her, and what his emotions on the inside were like. She knew that all this time. Something told her he wasn't soulless. Perhaps the reason she wanted to know as badly as she did was that her feelings towards him impaled her, demanding her to acknowledge them. But she wondered how it would be possible to love someone and be miserable if they didn't love her back. So it was really the fear of misery that drove her to ask him how he felt. But perhaps she didn't want to be as direct as she should in terms of how he felt about her specifically.

"What's up with that?" She decided to be cryptic, too.

"It's just how we are," he answered.

Vira nearly facepalmed herself. It annoyed her immensely how closed off he was. He wouldn't even give her a straight answer on anything.

"Cassius." Her voice grew loud. "So you're telling me you're just going to let everyone else decide?"

He seemed the type to be mad about underestimation, so she knew to push him in that direction.

"No, it's what I am spiritually, whether anyone told me or not."

"But these princesses who once lived. You didn't care to kiss them, or wrap your arms around their waist, or lay with them on the bed," she went on.

"Right, I'm soulless. I didn't care about intimacy with them," he answered.

"But you said it, that it was because that was *all* they wanted. And that they weren't beautiful inside, and that was why." Her stress rose.

"I suppose it was both things." He nodded his head in agreement.

"But you…" She was apprehensive to say it. It felt like a dam breaking loose inside of her when she said, "You kissed me, and you wrapped your arms around me, and you sat with me, all night on my bed," she cried.

Cassius stopped, looking down like he had just lost something. Vira stopped as well.

"That has to mean something, right? Or did you forget? Did you forget about the night we had together and how special that was to me? It happened the night I finished my painting, coming to terms with the fire inside of me that turned into joy that demands to burst out of me everytime I think of you."

Cassius shook his head slowly, turning it up to her, looking in her eyes. "No I didn't forget." He cocked his head. "Wait," he said. "You have…" He was taken aback, at a loss for words. "Feelings for me?"

"You're going to say it, aren't you? You're going to tell me exactly what you told me that night after it happened, how you don't want to be attached to me any more than you already are." She nearly got mad enough to draw a flame from her fingertips, but contained herself. "I've been trying to get out of you whatever you feel for me, all day. I feel impatient to know. Because I don't hide my feelings very well, and maybe that's my curse or not. But all I know is I'd say it loud and clear if it wouldn't get you killed back at my land. I have been happier these past days than I ever have in my life. For once, I don't feel alone in a room full of people. I feel something for someone. But most of all, it's a damned love that I wish more than anything else I could keep with me through the days and night of my existence."

"Vira!" he yelled.

She flinched back, as she had never heard his voice as loud as it was.

"You think I forgot about that night we spent together? No, I didn't. In fact, It's all I've been thinking about since it happened. I wish I could keep you here at the palace, and somehow tell the world you passed away. But I wouldn't do that to the people who love you, because I know what it's like to lose someone to death." He shook whatever anger he had out of him and stepped forward to Vira. "If you've learned anything about me, it's not that I don't have emotions, it's that they scare me. They scare me to feel, and they take over me like a virus."

Vira exhaled, nodding as she heard him talk. She didn't say anything in an attempt for him to keep talking and get to the point of how he really felt about her.

"But you..." He paused, seemingly trying to gather his thoughts, but there were too many of them to gather.

Vira's chest filled with excitement. Here was the moment she'd been waiting for a long time.

"You're the one I want. I used to think young love was an oxymoron. But you are the someone who took away the mental war I was in, battling it out in my head if I'd be better off dead like the others. But you showed me a reason to live. It pains me more than anything that I can't have you, Vira. Fate has a sick sense of humor sometimes."

Vira's eyes widened at the word *fate*. She knew he felt something for her, but she had no idea he thought they were fate. Perhaps they were, but perhaps their fate led them together in different directions. And it was indeed a sick, sick joke.

"You want me?" she repeated. "But you keep your emotions hidden because they're too strong?"

"It's a damned feeling. You're right." He nodded.

"Your emotions for me are too strong to let out because…"

"I'll quite literally explode," he finished her sentence.

"I want you, too." She looked into his deep eyes.

She could feel their bodies steadily gravitating closer and closer together as they stood facing each other. After not talking for a couple of seconds, Vira felt her eyes get heavy, watering from the tired feeling that turned her eyes red. But she could stare into his eyes all night and never get tired of it.

"Vira." His voice got softer. "You're tired."

He turned away just as their bodies almost touched and picked up a rose from the ground.

"I know." She nodded, yawning.

He turned to her with the rose and pulled her hand closer to him. With his other hand, he placed the ice rose into it, nodding with a soft smile. The rose itself was cold to the touch, just as Vira would expect it to be.

"Take it, even if you don't want it," he said as he let go of her hand.

Vira was too tired to respond at that point, so all she did was look down at the rose and softly smile.

He guided her into the doorway, then down the halls. It dawned on her that there hadn't been any beds in the Queen's room. At that, she wondered how she would get a goodnight's rest, sleeping on something that couldn't have been comfortable. After all, she couldn't blame Cassius. It was likely that vampires didn't know comfort, as he hadn't slept in decades, allowing him to forget about what it was like to need a cushy surface to lay on, especially with all the traveling they had done in the day. Even then, she had been awake for nearly twenty four hours, and the darkness was starting to turn lighter.

They stopped at another door. It wasn't the queen's room, but it looked just like all of the other doors that seemed to be bedrooms.

Once he opened it up, it was darker than the hallway had been. She wondered if he had even noticed. Still, she knew it was his room somehow, most likely because out of all of the rooms, he chose the one door to stop at in particular.

"Well, I think it goes without saying, you're probably dead tired by now," he broke the silence.

When she stepped in the room, her eyes were nearly closed and her mind was too foggy from the tiredness. She could only answer with a nod.

He walked her closer inside the room, and when he did, her vision could only vaguely make out a long, backless couch that sat in the center of his room. It looked better than sleeping on the floor or a table of some sort at least.

She put her hand on it, seating herself on it to avoid falling. It was still cushy, which took Vira by surprise.

"I'll just be in here, with you. It's been a while since I've been here. It might take a while for me to get used to it," he said.

Vira nodded again, laying all the way down on the couch and dropping her bag on the floor. Part of her went to sleep upset, because she knew her time with Cassius was coming to an end sometime soon. The only thing they had left to do after she woke up in the morning was head back to the palace and retrieve the crown. Only now, Vira knew exactly how she'd do it. But that didn't stop her eyes from fluttering and her entire body weakening, even though she dreaded waking up.

THE EARRING

As Vira's eyes opened, she was unable to tell the difference between night and day immediately. The room was still dark, darker than her room had ever been.

Vira stretched, nearly bumping a candle that was set out next to the couch she was laying on on the top of a side table. It was kind of Cassius to at least consider the fact that her vision mattered, too, and that she could barely see anything last night.

She lit it up after creating a flame with her hand and it lit nearly the entire room up, revealing Cassius was not there. Maybe that was a good thing so far, since she had just gotten used to being both at the Wintercastle Palace and in a man's room, which had never been the case prior for either of the scenarios.

His room wasn't blue like she had come to expect, but more of a neutral off-white mixed with silver for the detailing. Vira picked up the candle from the holder and stood up. After she let her eyes adjust to the light and waking up in general, she stepped towards the giant bookshelf that first caught her eye. It reminded her of the library back at the palace, the way the gold foiled spines stuck out and the shelf took up nearly the entire wall. She assumed he must have been a reader, and that he had a lot of knowledge. She found intelligence enticing, which added onto the things she liked about him.

She turned around, looking out to the rest of the room, noticing it was almost bare other than his closet, the couch and something she was unable to decipher from where she was standing. But it was large and took up nearly the entire side wall. She walked towards it, seeing that it was a mural. She stepped closer to it, noticing the image of a middle aged woman with longer blonde hair and rosy cheeks. It seemed odd that Cassius had a mural of a woman in his room, considering he never had loved a woman before and none of the vampire princesses appealed to him.

A velvet, buttoned chair sat next to it, black legs with deep red material. Something about the setup seemed abnormal to Vira. She knew he was closed off, but she really thought she had gotten somewhere last night with him. Apparently, there were some things about him she still didn't know anything about.

There wasn't much else of his room to see. Perhaps his closet was decent but there wouldn't be much to see in there. So she guessed it was time to find him. They did, in fact, need to get moving soon in order to get back to the palace before she was questioned any further about why she had been gone as long as she was.

She still held the candle stick with one hand and her bag with the other as she walked out the door. She made her way down the hallway she went to when Cassius walked her to his room. Minutes down the hall, still, nobody was to be seen. Which was a good thing, unless it was Cassius.

Anxiety struck her, remembering the last time she woke up expecting to see Cassius and didn't. He was gone for days. But this time, she knew he had to be somewhere in the palace. Her hands trembled a bit as she held the candlestick, but she knew not to worry too much this time.

The halls seemed to go in a circle, which worked to Vira's benefit. Therefore, she would run into him at some point. As she wandered the halls, her mind also wondered, guessing where he may be. Vampires don't eat, so there will be no chance that he could be in the dining room that most likely didn't even exist here. He doesn't sleep either, so he wouldn't have wandered off to find another couch. But he had to be somewhere. Where that was, Vira worried at least somewhat it wouldn't be a good place. She would have guessed he would have come to her by now when she saw a large clock on the wall, which had just struck nine o'clock. He ought to know she was awake by now. Or maybe he didn't know better. But he should have, considering he knew to give her a candle to light up the dark, as she could not see like he could.

She stopped and listened when she could hear the subtle voices that sounded faint from a distance. She knew he had to be near now. It sounded like his voice. It had to be his. But she wondered who he could possibly be talking to.

She proceeded to follow the voice and listen closely. It grew subtly louder as she came closer to it, approaching wherever Cassius was.

Soon, she reached where the sound was most prominent. She knew she just passed it when she heard it quiet down, but backed up several steps. Now she knew where the voice was coming from. There stood a window that resembled a glass gate and a door in the middle of it. It took up the entire wall, but when she peered through the crack of the door that seemed to lead to the outside as the light was brighter, she heard his voice loud and clear.

From the glimpse of Cassius she caught, he was facing an audience of some type. Vira had assumed it to be the nobles and mortals of the isle, and he was speaking to them like he mentioned the first time he left the palace. One thing she noticed was he had on his prince crown, which she had never seen before. It was soft black with red stones at the arches. His outfit was also different from what he previously had on. The top and pants were both black with accents of white for the buttons and rims. He was an attractive prince to Vira. Not that he hadn't always had the most appealing gaze and toned body when he stretched just the right way, but something about him the way he looked as a prince gave her extra butterflies right now.

She set down her bag on the floor gently by the wall and peered out into the see-through part of the wall looking out into the outside. He was on a platform attached to the palace like a balcony, and the others were gathered below.

Even when Vira stepped closer, concentrating on whatever he was announcing to them, she still couldn't decipher what he was saying. She held onto the wall as she peeked deeper out into the balcony. She even went as far to crack open the door little by little, wider to hear his echoing voice.

Her heart nearly dropped when something fell off of her head when she attempted to run her fingers through her hair. She realized then that her tiara was still fastened in her hair. Only now, it wasn't. It made its way through the travel to get here, and it stayed fastened while she slept. But it dropped to the floor, creating a ping noise that drew attention to her. Her face turned red when she picked it up, moving out of the way and acting as if nobody had seen her and nothing had happened. She was behind the wall now panicked, squeezing her eyes tight in embarrassment. She couldn't believe she had interrupted Cassius' announcement to the public. Even worse, some of the audience definitely saw her, even if the entire platform was dimmed by the shade the rest of the palace above casted on the platform.

She had hoped he didn't notice, but there was a good chance he at least heard it and had an idea. He didn't look back, but if some of the mortals noticed, so would he. She worried that she may have blown it somehow. Like she ruined something for him. The last time he was there making an announcement, he informed them he was, in fact, the only one left from the palace and the other ones were all defeated during the war. Now, they had to have known something else was up.

It was a shame that she still couldn't understand at all what he was saying to them. Perhaps she had walked in at the wrong time. A gust of wind blew the door closed, and Vira knew she wasn't going to crack it back open again.

Anxiety had hit her that, yet again, she had made a mistake by not staying in his room until he came back to her, even if she was never directed to by him. He never said not to, which would be her defense if he asked why she nearly ruined the announcement he was making.

The door opened again, and Vira's hands held each other tight to contain her nerves.

Cassius stopped, startled by her standing straight against the wall when he noticed her. He picked up the tiara and handed it to her with a grin.

"Sorry," she immediately said and took the tiara, feeling ashamed still.

"What happened?" He looked back at all the people exiting the palace audience.

"I don't know. I came to try and find you, and when I did, I accidentally dropped my crown from my head." She looked down at it in her hands.

"That was you?" he asked, concerned.

"Yes, and some of your people saw me," she said.

"How many?" His concern grew.

"I don't know…" She struggled to think. "Maybe the first row?"

His eyes grew wide as he started walking. Vira followed.

"Why didn't you just stay in the room?" he asked.

"I don't know. It was a while after that I found you here. The last time I woke up and hadn't seen you when I expected to, you were gone for days, so I panicked." Panic was, indeed, in her voice.

"Ah, I guess I forgot how long you guys slept for," he admitted. "Or not."

"Either way, I'm sorry. I probably ruined everything," she apologized again.

"There's no need to apologize," he said with a smiling laugh.

Vira cocked her head at him and said, "Huh?" It was a relief to know she didn't cause as much damage as she thought she did.

"The most I'll get is a dumb conspiracy theory made up about me." He swatted his hand in dismissal.

"Oh." She laughed it off, too. "I guess so."

"But we better get back to your palace," he said, looking unsure of himself as he saw the gleaming sun.

"Right, find your king crown so you can crown yourself king." She was clearly underwhelmed about it.

"Right," he repeated, matching her underwhelmed tone.

He walked a few steps before he stopped and his eyes grew wide. "Wait."

Vira looked back at him with concern. "Yes?"

"What is it that you want from here?" he asked.

Perhaps he was looking for ways to keep her there longer, thus, to be able to spend more time with her.

"I already got—" she started as she touched her necklace.

"No, that's not enough." He shook his head, eager for her to take something else.

"It's not?" she asked, crinkling her nose.

"No." He adamantly shook his head and took her hand, taking off down the hallway.

Vira didn't mind finding any and every excuse for them to spend time together, even if she was eager to get back to the palace for the peace and mind that everything hadn't gone to hell.

He stopped at the Queen's room, then opened the door.

"Wait right here," he demanded.

He walked fast paced inside of the room, then came out a minute later.

Whatever he had, his hands were over it and his arms were hiding it. He looked down at it with pride, but then showed it to her, revealing that it was a long chain with a diamond at the end of it. Vira still couldn't tell what it was, or the significance of it, but she didn't mind.

He waited for Vira to smile before nodding for her to come inside.

"Here, so you can see yourself." He motioned to the mirror when she walked in.

They both stood facing the mirror as Cassius stood to the side of her, just behind her. She watched him in the mirror as he moved her hair out of the way to reveal her ear. His cold touch made her already miss him and reminded her of how much they'd miss each other once their mission was over. The candle she held lit the scene just enough to give the scene a romantic glow, casting a subtle golden shadow among both of their faces.

It was now that Vira realized that what he had given her was an earring. But now that she knew what it was, it was gorgeous.

He grabbed her earlobe gently and slid the sharpness into her ear, holding onto her far shoulder with his other hand, seemingly for concentration. But Vira knew how he was with physical touch. Now that she knew he would have wanted to be with her if their fates took them in opposite directions, she could tell even by his intense gaze towards her alone that every single touch of his meant admiration, rather than convenience.

He stopped, allowing himself to be close to her for more than a few seconds after he had put the earring in her ear. His gaze danced around her neck, the closest part of her body his face had ever been without touching it.

"What?" Vira whispered, even though she didn't need to.

"Nothing, I just..." he spoke softly as he looked up at the mirror.

For a moment, they both looked in the mirror at themselves and into each other's eyes, smiling at the sight. Vira knew they looked like a perfect match, the way his eyes were like a soft blanket all over her when he looked at her. His brown hair complimented her deep red hair as they intertwined in each other when his face got closer to hers.

Vira still watched the mirror, but Cassius' gaze found its way back to her. It was their one last chance to be romantic before they got the king's crown, so every second counted.

But Vira's eyebrows drew in together when she looked closer to Cassius' face in the mirror. He looked like he was struggling with something. Perhaps he wanted more than anything to bite her, or kiss her, or maybe both. Which one, Vira couldn't decide just by looking at him.

"You alright, Cassius?" she asked.

But then, he looked like he could cry if it was possible.

"I don't know," he said. "Perhaps I can't hold in my emotions as well as I used to since I met you."

Vira turned to him, concerned. She set down the candle on the vanity and said, "Don't."

He looked up at her with big eyes.

"Don't hide your feelings," she demanded, shaking her head.

They were maybe six inches apart from each other, and as the seconds went by, the space got smaller.

"I don't know if it's a life worth living if I'm doing it all alone," he admitted.

"You said you didn't want to die, Cassius," Vira said, confused.

"I'll have this palace," he looked around, "all to myself, and everyone will think my life is greater than any of theirs." He shook his head in doubt. "But I want you. I do. Whatever it has to take, I'm willing to go through it."

Vira's eyes grew wide. "Are you sure this isn't just a temporary feeling?"

Cassius cocked his head.

"I mean, this is your first time, and mine, feeling this way for someone. Are you sure this won't go away for you after time passes?" she asked, paranoid that he'd say yes.

"Will it for you?" He seemed anxious to ask.

Vira paused in anticipation for a second. She exhaled, then shook her head. "No."

"I can't live for eternity, hundreds of years, with an entire palace and isle on my shoulders, and do it all alone." He meant it. "Vira, you are all I need. You're not the one I want. You're the one I need."

"And you are all I need." Vira realized her love for him. A single tear drop fell from her cheek.

Cassius gently wiped the tear from her cheek, causing her to look up into his eyes again.

"How are we going to do this?" Vira asked.

"I don't care what it takes." He sounded demanding. "If you have to run away, or fake your own death and hide deep within these castle walls for the rest of your life, I don't care."

Vira nodded her head in agreement. "Okay." She could only find the words to say.

"Okay?" he repeated with a smile on his face.

"Okay." Vira smiled and laughed.

"But first, we need to go back to the palace to get the crown. That should be the last thing we need to do, isn't it?" Cassius suggested.

Vira nodded, then said, "Yes, I know exactly where and how to find it."

"Everything has to go right this time, or we'll both be dead," he said.

"You're right," Vira realized. "We better go now."

They both made their way out the door and into the palace halls.

"This earring, was this the Queen's?" Vira asked.

"Actually, no." He shook his head. "My mother's. She was next in line for queen status."

Vira realized that she had never heard Cassius mention his mother before.

"Is that who was on your wall?" she asked.

"My wall?" he asked.

"Yes. The mural painting of a woman. She had golden blonde hair and rosy cheeks. It was in your room."

"Ah," he nodded his head. "My mother was, indeed, a vampire. She moved to the palace when I was young. I thought all that time she had left me until I found out she needed to for my safety."

"Your safety?" Vira wanted him to elaborate.

"Yes, like sorcerers and wolf shifters, us vampires are a secret society. Anyone who knew about us had to either die or become a vampire. My mother switched to be a vampire when I was young. She suffered from the same medical conditon as I had, scaring her into transforming. I thought she had died or something when I hadn't heard from her in ages, but it turned out she half died when she became a vampire, and moved to the palace to be one of the older princesses."

"When you came to the palace, you were grateful to know your mother was still around?" Vira asked, even if it wasn't necessary.

"I was thrilled. It was the greatest shock of my life, and I wish I could go back and see her again." He was passionate as he spoke.

"I'm sorry that she died in the war." Vira realized that when she said it.

"I would say I hate you and that I wish death upon you, but I know you differently now," he said. "See, the reason I ran towards you was because I saw you light her entire body on fire."

Vira's eyes grew wide and a cold, panic feeling began in her chest.

"You mean to tell me I was one of the people who helped in your mother's death?" She felt sick to say the words.

Losing her mother was one of the worst things to have ever happened to Vira. If not, the worst. And to know she caused the same pain upon Cassius shattered her on the inside.

"You did, yes." He nodded his head.

"What can I do?" It was beyond her to even ask.

"Nothing. My mother would have liked you. You're just like her in some ways," he said.

It put Vira in even more shock to hear him say.

"Cassius, no, I killed her." She shook her head in shame.

"But you saved me." He looked in her eyes as they walked to calm her. "And I was most important to her in the world."

"Man," Vira exhaled in grief. "It's hard to live with that."

"One of the things I had to get used to when I became a vampire was learning to live with my mistakes and failures," he comforted her. "And besides, you were just doing your job, protecting your people."

"You're right." Vira finally calmed down. "I didn't know any better."

Something still radiated through Vira that was worse than guilt. Even if she had no intention of kiling his mother, she was now wearing her earring, and saw her face back when her head was still attached to her body.

They finally reached the palace doors.

Vira stopped as she saw the sunlight. "Wait," she said.

Cassius stopped as well in the shade and looked back at her.

"Why just one earring?" she asked.

"You did tell them you lost *an* earring, didn't you?" He smiled.

Vira nodded in realization. "Ah."

"That's the earring you lost." Cassius winked.

For a moment, they both laughed it off.

But after, Cassius stood still, looking out into the sunny area while he still stood in the shade.

"What?" she asked as if she didn't know.

"I don't know what to do."

Vira opened the bag she was holding and handed him the guard hat.

"I don't get to know what happens to you in the sun, I'm guessing?" she asked sarcastically.

Cassius took the hat and said, "Thank you." he fastened it on his head and said, "I'm sensitive to it." He tilted it upright.

Vira proceeded to take out more of the guard uniform and nodded for him to go on as he took it, sliding it on over the vampire prince outfit.

"If we get too much of it, we could burn," he explained.

"A sunburn?" Vira joked.

Cassius laughed subtly. "No," he said. "If I'm out in the sunlight for too long, it could burn my skin off."

"I suppose now I'm not as curious to see it." Vira laughed as they walked out into the open sunlight once Cassius was covered.

They approached the tiny life boat they rode to the isle on. It was still there, bobbing up and down as the waves rolled in and out.

It wasn't far out into the water, so Cassius reached out long to drag it almost all the way onto the land. Cassius stepped in first, then sat down, then Vira followed. When she attempted to sit down, she was the good kind of startled when she accidentally sat on his lap.

"Sorry." She blushed as she moved up a bit, parking herself on the boat part.

As Cassius pushed them back into the ocean, he leaned in and spoke low. "No need to apologize."

From the way his voice sounded, he would have been blushing too if he had blood in his system to turn his cheeks rosy red

The first part of the ride, they sat in silence. Vira's stomach fluttered, being in between his legs, exactly where she wanted to be. It was the perfect place at the perfect moment. It would be even more perfect, however, if they weren't on the way to Siciland Palace. It was too bad that she could only feel his legs in front of her as he sat there, squeezing them together on her as he maneuvered the boat with the oar in the water to paddle them back to land.

"What was your announcement to the nobles?" Vira asked, half to break the silence and half because she was curious.

"I told them I've found the king's crown, and there will be a crowning ceremony soon where I crown myself king by default," he explained.

"Ah," Vira nodded. "So they're eager, huh?"

"They are." Cassius sounded sure of it. "They're worried about the isle. They feel like something bad is going to happen with nobody in power since our monarch system has gone to hell."

"I wouldn't blame them," Vira replied. "Who are they without their king?"

"It's a lot to handle being king, I don't know how well I'll adjust." It was clear Cassius was apprehensive by the sound of his voice.

"You'll do just fine," Vira attempted to comfort him.

"Alone?" he asked. "I just don't know how I'm going to do it."

"You're awesome. I just know you'll find a way," she encouraged.

Vira could only hear a snicker from Cassius' as a response.

It was too bad that the island was already near. They hadn't spent much time talking, but maybe just enjoying the moment with him was enough for Vira to appreciate. It was more so heading back to the palace that caused her unease. Talking to her step father wouldn't be easy, and hiding her emotions would be even more difficult. But some of her peace of mind came from knowing they would plot another secret escape sometime soon. One that would be forever.

The only person she would feel guilty for lying to was Altha. Altha lost both of her parents, and if one of her best friends passed away, or so she would believe, may just push her over the edge. And Vira would never be able to see Altha again. Some second thoughts arose the closer they had gotten to the island and even more came about when they pulled up.

Vira gulped as she stepped out of the boat once it was on dry land. She wondered if the hard and fast decision would even work out.

"You go that way." She pointed to the woods where they would regularly meet. "And I'll go through the front." She pointed in the other direction.

The last thing they needed was to be seen together and busted on the spot.

"Sounds like a plan." Cassius smiled before taking off to avoid being seen with Vira now that they were on Siciland ground.

CAPTURED

Once Vira reached the front gate of the palace, nerves settled their way in. She worried immensely of the first encounter she would have with her step father. She also worried for Cassius and if anyone had noticed anything strange yet. If anything, she hoped Altha would have covered it up somehow for her.

It was obvious that Cassius would have been to the palace by now, as he had moved faster than Vira from what she observed earlier when he carried her long distances.

But as she walked the palace halls, he was nowhere to be seen yet. Perhaps he was still by the garden waiting for her to show up, or maybe he was pretending to sleep at the guard bunks.

It wasn't past noon yet, it was closer to half past eleven, so it was promising that nobody had even noticed their disappearance. As far as Vira's step father was concerned, Vira had spent the night with Altha anyways.

With every step Vira took, her suspicion and unease grew, however. The silence that kept in the halls struck her as alarming. For this far into the day, it was unusual for the palace.

The main thing on her mind was finding Cassius for the sake of peace in mind. However, when she thought of him, she also felt regretful at what she had done and made plans to do with him once she retrieved the king's crown.

"For sake, Vira," a masculine voice came from out of nowhere. "You could at least have told me."

Vira's heart dropped and her stomach went cold as she looked around frantically in search of the voice.

"Vira!" Altha came running around the corner. "Vira! Vira!" she called out again.

Altha approached her with a mortified look on her face.

"What is it?" Vira asked.

"Your lover, he's been captured, they're at the other back of the palace." She sounded panicked.

"What?" Vira yelled as she ran.

Altha ran after her as well. She looked back, seeing that it was one of the many guards who had spoken before Altha had come around the corner. It seemed to also have been the one who caught them coming out of Vira's room.

Vira's eyes grew wide as she glanced back at the guard once more, noticing that he was holding the crown that Cassius had been looking for all along. Part of her wanted to turn around and take it back from him, but it was more important that she get to Cassius to see him at least one last time. The guard seemed to be headed the same way Vira and Altha were.

"What happened?" Vira struggled to say as she ran.

"You'll see." Doubt filled Altha's voice as she replied.

As they approached the scene, the silence went away and the noise became louder.

It was a challenge to decipher what exactly was going on with all of the guards standing by. She could only catch a glimpse of the peak of her stepdad's head at the top.

Once her stepdad noticed them approaching, he stepped to the front.

"Elvira," he said with a straight face. "Where were you last night?"

"I was with Altha, helping with their house." She gulped as she spoke.

"Strange that Altha did, indeed, come to the palace last night to care for Aleski," he said.

Vira suddenly felt like a sharp dagger impaled her chest.

"What?" she said as she felt like she was going to throw up.

"That's right, she needed to tend to his starved and freezing cold body. He then told me everything."

It was hard to understand why he had almost no emotion when he spoke. Perhaps he was the soulless one.

But Vira was only worried about Cassius and where he was if he was alive. She didn't care about the fact that she was busted now.

"Where…" she struggled to say, but then worked up the anger to yell, "is Cassius?"

The crowd lowered in noise and several of the guards back over at Vira and her step father talking. She assumed they had just noticed her.

Her stepdad turned to them and said with a grin, "You heard her, boys, show him."

Several guards moved out of the way to reveal two of them holding Cassius, one on each side of his arms. His hat was taken off his head, revealing his face and his hair was hanging down in front of his eyes with a look of defeat. He looked up at Vira with a look of nothing but sorrow.

Vira gasped and her eyes grew wide. "Let him go!" she yelled as if it would do anything. It hurt her worst of all to see him detained by men of the palace, or for him to be defenseless with his arms out of his control. The fire inside her radiated heavily enough it felt like she could burst into flames any second.

Several of the guards laughed, which was the only answer she had gotten.

"I said, let him go!" she yelled even louder.

Vira took a chance as she lunged into the crowd of guards, but she knew it was over for her when one of the guards restrained her by taking her arms in his.

"You better not hurt her." Cassius looked up at the man who was holding Vira back with the most grim look she'd ever seen on his face.

The guards didn't say a word.

It was mainly because, shortly after, Vira's step father said, "Ah, here we have it."

The guards made their way, stepping to the side with Vira and Cassius in their restraint as the guard Vira saw earlier came through and stepped into the scene. He was still holding the king's crown with both hands, leaving Vira confused.

Vira cocked her head as she watched him step in front of Cassius with a look of amusement on his face, like whatever he was about to do was entertaining to him.

It was seconds before Vira found out why. The guard's face grew tight, like he was lifting something heavy. Then, the crown smashed inward, shattering into hundreds of tiny pieces, clinking as they hit the floor.

Vira's heart stopped as she gasped, realizing all that she had done was now lost, and the trouble they had gone through was all for nothing. Vira wanted to cry in frustration, but when she looked up at Cassius, he didn't even look like he wanted to frown. He had a straight face, like the crown all of a sudden meant nothing to him.

It left Vira confused as to how he could be as emotionless as he was when he lost everything he had longed for. Perhaps he was only trying to hide his emotions and put up the cold, soulless front he had the entire time with her up until she shook it out of him, but it seemed genuine from what Vira could infer.

Vira looked down at all of the smashed pieces of crown on the floor, realizing that it was somewhat dumb on their part to smash it where they'd need to clean it up.

The guard suddenly let Vira go. She jerked away from him with spite and looked over at Cassius. It felt like it would be the last time that they'd look into each other's eyes.

His mouth hung open and seemed to mouth the words *I'm sorry*. His face surely gave off those words even if his mouth didn't the way his forehead crinkled and his eyebrows hung low. But Vira didn't know what he was apologizing for.

One of the guards retaining Cassius loosened his grip as he seemed to lose focus after such a long time. But Cassius took the chance and slipped through their arms while he could.

Before her eyes, Vira watched him lunge near her quickly. Within the second she had to think, she assumed it was to kiss her one last time, which would be her hope. Or to take her with him wherever he went. Or if it was to tell her something, anything.

But the second passed, and before Vira could even blink, one of his hands was on her shoulder and the other one moved her hair out of the way like he had done at the palace earlier before slipping the earring on. Instead of kissing her, or whispering something in her ear, perhaps that he loved her, she felt his teeth sink into her neck in a piercing motion.

Vira's eyes grew wide as soon as it had all sunk in. The hallway was now filled with chanting noise from the guards to catch him immediately, but Cassius used his speed abilities to escape into what seemed like thin air.

Vira held her neck in pain. But it hadn't been nearly as painful as what she had imagined. She could feel the torn muscle everytime she moved, but the pain was only mild.

"Altha, take her and fix her," Vira's stepfather ordered.

Altha froze, then panicked as she said, "I can't."

"Why not?" His voice grew louder over the sound of the guards running around looking for Cassius even though Vira knew they'd never catch him. He was far too strategic, despite how he went about handling Aleski.

"I don't have the proper equipment to handle a vampire bite, and look, it didn't even seem to do anything to her." Altha motioned to Vira.

And she was right. Even Vira was confused as to how she wasn't on the floor screaming in pain from the vampire venom radiating throughout her entire body. She held her arms out in front of her and observed that they hadn't changed color, nor felt any bit different. She held her hand to her heart as she could still feel it beat.

"You're right, it's not," her step father agreed.

He whistled with his fingers, beckoning two of the guards. Altha's nerves grew again, but not nearly as bad. It was like something was blocking her nerves from spinning out of place.

"Take her away," he ordered.

Without a second going by, the two men grabbed Vira by the arms and started waking her down the hallway.

"And detain her," her step father yelled extra loud.

Vira wasn't surprised he'd call for detainment, but it was even more of a shock to herself that she willingly walked as they brought her to her cell within the palace.

DETAINED

Vira was half glad that Cassius had gotten away. At least he had a better chance of surviving now for all she knew. And it seemed like that was all that mattered to her at this point.

But what Vira stressed more about was the fact that she wasn't feeling any symptoms of being injected with his venom.

She didn't know who she let down more: Cassius or herself. Somehow, she believed it was herself. Mainly because she had the chance to do the right thing and avoid everything that had happened. But her love for him grew overtime and it was inevitable to grow attached to him. It was a new feeling for her, a feeling she had never gotten, which was all she could ponder now.

But now she had nobody at all, so none of it mattered anymore. Cassius was supposedly alive and Vira was alive, but she didn't know if that mattered either at this point. She wondered if she'd be better off dead.

Vira hated what her life had come to as she sat in the cell for hours staring at a wall, pondering what she'd do with herself now or if she'd ever be able to leave this life of loneliness.

"Miss Rossi," a man's voice said.

The cell was dark enough to make Vira stand up and squint her eyes as she held the prison bars. She leaned her head on them to be able to see who had spoken.

It was one of the guards, an indecipherable one at that.

"Yes?" she excitedly answered.

She thought it could be that she'd be able to leave the cell, finally, or that she could finally have something to eat. At this point she was starving.

"Someone is here to see you," he informed her.

Vira's eyebrows drew together in confusion. She wondered who it could possibly be. For sure, it couldn't have been her step father. Now, she was sure he wanted nothing to do with her. Her best bet was that it was Altha. Out of everyone, she'd be the one most likely to visit her while she was detained.

"Who is it?" Vira asked as the guard jingled the keys, finding the right one then unlocking her cell.

Immediately, he tied her up in handcuffs so she wouldn't escape his arms like she previously had.

He only shrugged in response, which seemed peculiar to Vira, considering the guard would have known if it was Altha.

Question and confusion filled Vira's mind as the guard walked her out to another room, equally bolted up as the last.

When he opened the door, the woman who sat on the other side of the table she was about to be seated at looked no bit familiar to Vira.

Vira looked back, confused at the guard as he released his hands from her. He shoved her from behind the rest of the way in the room forcefully, then closed the door behind her.

"Hello." Vira stepped forward in concern as she took a seat.

The woman had long, blonde hair and her cheeks were rosy red, similar to the picture she had seen in Cassius' room, but in another life.

"Vira, Vira Rose?" she asked in question. "Is that your name?"

Vira nodded as her mouth hung open in concern. "Vira Rossi. But yes, that is my name."

"I've been forcefully called to speak with you," the young woman said with a strikingly straight face.

"You have?" Vira asked. "Who are you?"

"I'm one of the newest sorcerers. I've just been inducted," she explained. "My sorcery allows me to see the future," she said as she held up a jar of golden dust.

"Ah," Vira nodded, still confused.

"I was on a leisurely walk around the palace this morning, and when I walked past the back where the dungeon is, something almost impaled me to reach you," she went on. "It's safe to say most people who live near the palace either saw first hand or heard what happened this morning. And I was among one of them. But I have more to say to you."

"Everyone knows about it now?" Vira's eyes grew wide and her heart felt like it sank down into her stomach. She wasn't surprised, though, that yet another thing had happened that made her want to curl up in a ball and hide forever until her bones turned to ash.

The young lady nodded and said, "But I have something even more important to tell you." Her voice went serious. "I know you're a friend of Altha's. She told me. But what I need to tell you is that a friend of Altha's is also someone who I wouldn't mind helping as well."

Vira nodded, as if it made sense to her why this woman would care for the now most hated woman on the island all of a sudden.

"What's going on?" Vira was eager to know.

"Well I did a read for you, and it shows that if you don't leave now and flee to Wintercastle Isle, death is in your near future," she said after taking a breath.

"Death? How am I supposed to get out of here?" Vira almost yelled, holding up her chained up wrists.

"My reads don't tell me anything. After all, it is just flying dust that turns itself into a picture, but I felt compelled to tell you, and I don't happen to wish death upon you," she explained.

Vira's heart thumped and thumped. She nodded frantically and her face filled with anxiousness. She felt herself sweat from her face down.

Vira touched the vampire bite on her neck as much as she could in the handcuffs, remembering that it was still there.

"Thank you," she pleaded. "I need to get out of here somehow." She looked around as if that would help her escape.

"You better. I know what you did and I don't agree with it at all, but Altha still cares for you, and I care for her. I could sense how she feels bad for you."

Vira only answered with a sign and a nod as she looked to the floor.

She knew she better get used to it. First, it was herself who she hated and felt that she made too many mistakes. Now, everyone hated her. But hate wasn't her top priority right now. It was surviving.

BITE OF THIRST

I f it hadn't been for the simple fact that Vira needed to flee to Wintercastle in order to survive, she wouldn't have cared to. But now, she was back in her cell, planning her escape if there was even a way.

It would be time for her one meal soon, which meant the guard would be back any minute to take care of dinner matters.

But as soon as she thought of food, even the greatest pastries they served at the palace or her favorite pork, she wasn't hungry. In fact, she didn't even feel the need to eat anything despite the fact that she hadn't eaten all day.

But a wave of thirst hit her. She felt like a fish gasping for air, except she craved a beverage of some type. When she attempted to ponder what that beverage she had all of a sudden craved this bad, nothing specific came to mind.

The door opening caught Vira's attention. Her insides felt shriveled as she looked up at the guard who had just come through the doorway.

Vira rushed to the bars, then held them tight as she looked up at the guard who was carrying a brown paper bag of some type.

He met her at the cell.

"Hungry, huh?" he joked.

Vira didn't respond. She didn't think to. He seemed to think she was starving for whatever food was in the brown paper bag, but she was more so focused on the guard himself, and his flesh that showed in only a few places where the uniform hadn't covered.

The guard attempted to slide the paper bag through the bars, but it didn't quite fit. Vira stepped back, waiting for him to reach his hand accidentally too far into her cell towards her reach.

He grunted as he pushed the food even further. But still, it wouldn't fit.

"Wait there, just a moment," he said as he held a finger up at her and then took out his keys, using one hand to find the key to unlock the cell.

Vira's thirst grew exponentially. Her eyes went grim and her entire body started to shake at the idea of gripping her hands onto him in a strangle. Her hands shook even worse as she looked down at them, noticing their sudden discoloration, and the feeling of thirst persisted and got worse by the second. Her eyelids stayed open the entire time and from what she could tell, they drooped dark over her vision, like they turned a black color.

The guard held the key upward as he struggled to jiggle it in the lock to open it and hold the bag of food at the same time.

It came undone seconds later, and by then, Vira didn't know whether she was hungry or thirsty. One thing she knew was that she was desperate for whichever it was.

"Here," said as he stepped foot into the cell, holding the bag out to her. "This is all you get."

As Vira came closer to him, she felt a rush of eagerness. She ran up to him with a look of hunger. As she approached him, she reached her arms out to him. The guard seemed unalarmed, as if Vira was only dying of hunger for the food he had in the paper bag, but little did he know that wasn't the case.

Without another breath, she latched her canines onto his neck and inhaled deeply as she began sucking the blood from him. It was sweet and salty both at once, but it also had almost no taste. Vira wondered how she craved it, as badly as she did, with how unappetising it both sounded and tasted.

The sound of the guard squealing penetrated Vira's ear drums, nearly causing her to lose her hearing, but it didn't matter. The blood satisfied her too much to stop. In fact, she feared at that moment that she wouldn't be able to stop. But it was lucky for the both of them that Vira had a small stature and could only hold so much blood in her system.

So Vira let him go after a short time. When she did, he dropped to the floor, clearly in pain. He was breathing still, heavily at that, but the grimace on his face showed that he would be in pain for a while.

She knew now what she needed to do immediately. And she needed to make it fast before something else happened, losing her chance.

Vira noticed the dagger from his belt had clinked as it hit the floor, and that she could make good use of it if she took it for her escape. So she picked it up and used the other hand to wipe the blood from around her face.

Surely if anyone had spotted her along the way of fleeing to Wintercastle Isle, they'd be frightened to see her with a dagger, making her less approachable. It was normally only the guards who had them in the first place.

As she ran out of the back door that was still open from when the guard came through it to deliver the lunch, it was an instant relief. Both of leaving the cell and from the blood she had just consumed. It was an odd feeling to say the least. She could have been a murderer just then, but she wasn't able to stick around to find out if the guard would recover or not. At that, she now had yet another regret.

She made her way farthest away from the palace, which led to the area where Maycaster and Davelburn joined, which was also where the war had taken place. But she knew she needed to go as north as she could in order for nobody to see her anywhere, even with binoculars.

As Vira ran north, her speed got faster and it was all of a sudden easier to run the distance in a short amount of time. It was likely from the vampire bite, but something still didn't seem right to Vira. She wasn't quite a vampire yet, and she wasn't quite rid of her flame sorcery.

When she made it to the shore, she was at a loss for what to do next. At least nobody was near, and at least nobody was out to get her that she was aware of yet.

From a distance, she had seen a small lifeboat sunk down in the water most likely from the war when the vampires traveled to the island. So she dove into the water to retrieve it in order to row herself to the island. She opened her eyes in the water, breathing air out of her nose to keep herself steady. It was surely a good thing that the water was clear enough to see.

The first thing she was able to see was the wooden boat, which she used a great amount of strength to pick up out of the sand it was embedded in.

After it arose to the surface after a few hard tugs, she couldn't believe her eyes. From underneath the boat floated a crown. And not just any crown, but it surely seemed like only the crown a king would wear. Perhaps now it made sense that Cassius hadn't let out any emotions as the other crown was destroyed right in front of his face. He had to have known that wasn't the king's crown.

Vira realized her breath wasn't going to hold much longer, so she swam up to the surface of the water, breathing deep for air after she came up as she held onto the boat to keep herself up.

She picked up the vampire king's black crown and admired it for a moment. It was surely expensive, with ruby stones as the detail and the white velvet that would surely look gorgeous once cleaned and dried. As soon as it sunk in that she had found it, suddenly a weakening sensation went throughout her entire body. She even struggled to flip the small boat over and hop inside of it. It was a shame that she didn't have Cassius there to help her like he had last time. It would have come easier to her if he was.

She dropped the crown inside the boat and moved the wet hair out of her face. The sun beamed down on her, making her stomach curl. It was strange as it had never happened before. Luckily, she didn't need to reach far for the oar that also floated to the top of the water as she began to paddle her way to the isle.

As she reached a few feet out into the ocean, anger struck her when she saw bodies and remnants of vampires floating around in the ocean. It disturbed her more than anything she had ever seen in her life.

As she rowed herself, occasionally she had to push them out of the way in order to concentrate and make her way where she knew she needed to be unless she wished death upon herself. After everything she had been through, it was surely a surprise she didn't. Mainly because of Cassius and her longing to be with him. It made the entire trip there more than difficult.

Something strange began to happen inside Vira's body as she reached the middle of the ocean. Her skin grayed unpleasantly and she felt like she could drop any second. Perhaps it was also the sun beaming down on her that was stimulating something bad. It was a struggle to push through in order to get where she needed to be. The tint had only gotten worse over time and she felt no other way than she could simply explode. It fueled anxiety inside of her that she didn't know what was happening to her, and that perhaps this was what the future-telling sorcerer meant when she mentioned death would come in the near future.

Much of Vira's mind doubted she would even make it to the palace alive. But she kept pushing even when she felt like she could give out any second.

FALLING

Vira could see the palace when she struggled to look up. She knew now that she couldn't give up at this point. She refused death for as close as she was to getting to him.

There seemed to be too many mortals around for her liking near the palace, even if they looked like ants.

Her knees wobbled as she stepped out of the boat and onto the land. A wave of dizziness hit her when she started walking again.

It felt like she was dragging pounds of weight with every step she took. She held the crown gripped in her hands because if not, she knew she'd drop it, and it would be tragic to have made it to the island and broken it at the tail end of her journey.

"Cassius!" she yelled up at the palace as if he could hear her over the hundreds of thousands of mortals who were waiting for him to come out onto the platform.

Not having seen him yet made her very nervous. She wondered if he had even made it back to the isle.

With every step she took towards the palace, her breath grew heavier. But she still persisted to yell, "Cassius!"

She approached the back side of the palace where she knew to go in through, instead of the front where everyone else was. It would sure be damned if she came all this way just to die and not see him at least once.

The gated door opened when she approached it, almost as if it knew who she was and how much she had hoped Cassius wanted her there.

As soon as she entered the palace, she yelled his name again.

"Cassius!" It took all her might to say.

Vira thought indefinitely that it would be the end for her at that moment. She let out a one big cough and dropped to the floor shortly after all of her might escaped her body forcibly. The crown went down with her to the floor along with the dagger, clinging as they fell, but only bouncing, luckily without a single chip in it from the fall. She was half conscious as she laid there, but seconds later, she finally heard something.

"Vira!" Cassius' voice yelled as he came racing around the corner.

He must have ran from the other side of the palace to get to her as soon as he saw her approach the palace.

The last thing Vira knew happened was his hand lying on her face, whispering to her, "It's okay, queen. I've got you."

She could barely lift a finger or make out anything with her eyes. Her vision speckled subtly until it all went black.

PROPOSAL

Sunlight glistened into the room Vira had woken up in. Almost immediate, she was struck with the ache from everything that had happened within the past day. But she was just happy to wake up at this point.

Wherever she was, there was sound. She could only decipher it to be the subtle chanting of a crowd of people. So she let her eyes rest a second longer before opening them.

She was nowhere near ill like she had been the last time she was conscious, which she felt relief at, creating a smile on her face.

When Vira opened her eyes, it was clear to her that she was somewhere upon the hallway of Wintercastle Palace, laying down on the backless couch she had slept on the last time she found herself in the palace. She held out her arms and as she observed them, it struck her with disbelief. Her skin was already back to its natural color.

Behind her looked to be some type of a medical machine with a tube attached to it. She had no idea what it had been for, but she was sure it had something to do with why she even woke up in the first place.

She nearly hopped up as she ran to the near mirror, moving her hair from her neck to see that the vampire marks were just barely there. They looked to have closed up almost all of the way and soon nothing would be left of it

Just down the hall was an open area where the light seemed to seep in the most.

The thought of Vira's hero, Cassius, struck her mind. She needed to find him, to thank him for saving her from everything. Even the vampire bite saved her, and she had just now realized why he did it. It would eventually bring her back to him.

The noise grew louder as Vira rounded the corner of where it had all been coming from. The distant noise was the same as the last time Vira came searching for Cassius in the palace when she had woken up.

She felt the top of her head, touching her crown to make sure it was still on her head. And surprisingly, it still held strong.

Vira peered through the large widow, attempting not to draw too much attention to herself. Nobody seemed to notice her, but perhaps it was more so because she was too busy noticing Cassius standing strong and tall on the platform holding the king's crown. It was, indeed, the real king's crown.

His stature gave off an attitude of pride, which Vira was joyed to see.

After watching him for a few moments and being unable to decipher what words he was speaking out into the crowd of people, he raised the crown up towards the sky. Even though he was in the shade, more so because he had to be, it sparkled from the top.

As Vira looked out into the crowd of thousands of people, she noticed something had changed. The urge to suck their blood until they were dry vanished from her body. It seemed strange to her. But it also wasn't something to complain about. Just the thought of how she drank the guard's blood nearly made her sick to think of it now. Bile washed up her throat even at the thought of blood that reminded her tastebuds of the odd flavor.

Cassius lowered the crown, then placed it on his head. It had become clear to Vira that he had just crowned himself the King of Wintercastle. The crowd cheered for him, and Vira did the same behind the scenes. The mortals were now safe and their isle was at least getting to be a normal place again, allowing them the peace in mind. But Cassius had less of a victory. He didn't seem all that enthusiastic about becoming king. Proud, but not enthusiastic. At least, Vira seemed to pick up on it.

After the ceremony concluded with a bow from Cassius and a wave, he turned around to the door. His face lit up as soon as he saw Vira. Vira's face was already filled with delight, but to be with him now made it greater.

Cassius had never run faster as he came through the doors to approach Vira.

"You woke up," he cheered, more excited than Vira had ever seen him.

Vira answered only with a nod and smile. It was beyond words how euphoric she felt.

"It worked!" he cheered, holding her face and looking deep into her eyes.

"I know," Vira nodded. "What? You didn't think it would?"

Cassius paused and looked into her eyes before saying, "Remember when I said I thought I had a gift?"

Vira nodded, placing her hands on his shoulders. He immediately pulled her in closer.

"It was that I could save someone, and that person was you," he spoke softly as he said.

"You make me happier than I ever thought I could be," was the only thing Vira could think to say. "Congratulations, king."

She could tell in his eyes that it underwhelmed him to be called *king*.

"If you want to be called that," she added. "You are happy with it, are you?"

Cassius let out a brief chuckle, then said, "You know how I always call you queen?"

Vira nodded in realization. She knew even before he said another word what he was about to say.

"It was because, all along, I only wanted to live to be king if..." He seemingly struggled to ask, the way his voice went shy and nervous with a smile. "You'd be my queen?"

Vira's heart fluttered and suddenly his body felt like it could float.

"You..." Now it was her turn to choke on words. "You want me to be your queen?"

Cassius nodded, but was seemingly nervous that Vira would reject him.

Vira exhaled in excitement as she said, "Yes."

Cassius somehow lit up even more when she answered, leaning into her even more without a second of taking his eyes off her.

Vira took his hands from her face and moved them to her waist, then placed her hands onto his cold cheeks, wrapping herself up in him as their lips pressed hard against each other, leaving Vira breathless. He pressed his hands deeper into her hips, enough for her to be able to feel it through her dress, seeping into her bare skin. He leaned her back like a true queen, which was who she wanted to be for now on. Perhaps *flame princess* wasn't her unofficial name anymore. For now and on, she'd go by *flame queen*. And at that, she loved being the queen to the man she knew she'd continue to fall for until the rest of time.

BUT WAIT, THERE'S MORE!

TURN THE PAGE TO TO READ AN EXCERPT FROM THE SEQUEL, *QUEEN OF FLAMES*

PROLOGUE

THE LETTER

W hat didn't hit Vira right away when she left Siciland was what she had left behind. It wasn't her royalty, it wasn't all her gems, nor was it even the painting she painted of her and Cassius. It was Altha. Her dearest friend.

What Vira was left to ponder was the possibility that Altha had gone down with her when she was caught helping the vampire, who they wished death upon.

Vira loved Cassius, and she believed it even stronger now. But it created angst inside of her at the thought that

Altha could have gotten in deep waters if they had even suspected that she helped Vira in any way. But technically, she did when she covered for her when she informed the ruler she was helping with their house building. Altha was now worthy of the deadly punishments, too. In the sorcerer's society, one mistake could ruin their life. It wasn't often that they'd get a pass.

Vira's hand started to shake vigorously as she lifted a glass of water to her mouth to sip.

What have I done? she thought.

Cassius was now the king of the isle, which meant good things for Wintercastle. It was also the home isle of Vira now, which ultimately meant good things for her as well. A weak empire would call for invasion, if Vira learned anything from past events, and they were certainly in no place for invasion.

Vira was soon to be queen of Wintercastle, which excited her more than anything had ever excited her before. For once, she'd have control over something. Now, it would be almost everything.

But part of her wondered if being crowned queen would blow their cover, and that she'd no longer be able to keep a low profile. Surely, she wondered, *how were the others to know?*

Cassius walked into his room, where Vira was relaxing. More so, trying to.

"Can I get you anything, my queen?" he asked as he approached her, kissing the side of her face softly in admiration.

"I'm good." She masked her worries with a smile.

"Alright, I'm here," he answered. "When you get hungry, I'll order some food from the bakery in the town nearby."

Vira nodded with a smile as she took another sip of her ice water. She found lately that ice water was the only thing that would shock her fiery insides that heated up as her anxiety rose due to the stress, which happened a lot lately.

"Cassius," Vira called out as she reached her arms out in front of her, observing them. Question upon question arose from the day prior, leaving Vira wondering what had happened to her the day before and how she had even woken up, better yet, survived.

"Yes, queen?" he answered.

"Yesterday when I woke up, I felt fine," she said. "But before I fell to the floor, I felt like I could die nearly any second."

Cassius nodded, then stepped towards her to sit next to her on the same backless couch Vira had found herself on several times already.

"See, Vira," he explained. "When I bit you, it didn't agree with your insides because you were still a sorcerer."

"So what happened?" Vira asked him to elaborate.

"Well, your insides are warm and fiery, your veins flow fire through them practically, while my venom wanted to freeze it, like how it would stop a normal human's blood from flowing normally since they don't need it anymore. I had to suck the venom out of you," he explained.

Vira could feel her insides, and the more she thought about it, the more she realized she was no longer part vampire.

"Wow." She was taken aback. "I never knew that could happen."

It was clear that by nature, Cassius and her were opposites. She was fire and he was ice. Sometimes it worked, like the satisfying sensation Vira had gotten when she was intimate with him. And other times, it did nothing but destroy.

"When I laid you down on your bed after sucking you of the venom, I heard subtle breathing sounds coming from your mouth when I laid my head upon your chest. I knew there would be some hope that you'd come back," he explained.

"You didn't think I would make it?" Vira's eyes widened.

Cassius shook his head. "It had been a week before you had even woken up, but I knew I wouldn't forget about you." It seemed like it pained him to say. "Over time, your skin lost the gray pigment, and your natural glow came back. That's how I knew you were getting healthier."

It shocked Vira the most to learn she hadn't been unconscious for a day, but an entire week. She could have died. She was probably seconds away from it once she reached the palace.

"What would you have done if I died?" Vira's voice raised.

Cassius' face filled with guilt. "I would have never forgiven myself." He shook his head. "I probably wouldn't have crowned myself king, then I'd expose myself to the public for all to see, then go back to the palace, break the news, and allow them to take my life."

Vira gulped. "Wow." It had all sunk into her that more had happened than she thought.

"I understand if you regret agreeing to be crowned my queen." His face filled with sorrow as he spoke.

Vira snapped out of her own pity and sat up straighter. "No." She shook her head with a smile. "It's the one thing I won't regret doing."

"You won't?" Cassius grew a smile as soon as he saw hers. "How come?"

"Because. All my life, I've been told by other people how I should live. I can decide now and I will," she said with a demanding tone.

Ultimately, being crowned the queen of Wintercastle would grant Vira power of choosing her own lifestyle without the tedious instruction of others. Nobody would even be around to tell her otherwise. And most of all, it was only up from here, as she had finally found a place of belonging.

"We'll be deciding on a crowning date shortly. Surely your ceremony will have ten times the extravagance as mine did." He grinned.

"Surely?" Vira chuckled. "Cass, you crowned yourself, and you were the only other one on the platform when you did it."

His laugh mimicked hers. "I know, lame."

"I'm more than happy to start this journey together. Just the two of us, and a palace all to ourselves for now."

"And nobody to tell us no." He smiled softly.

His smile rubbed off on Vira, giving her the butterflies. Somehow, he still made her feel the same way even after all they had been through together.

"That reminds me, my queen, I'll be back. I have a room to set up for you." He ended his sentence with a wink.

Vira looked around at the surroundings in his room. "You mean to tell me this isn't going to be my room, too?" She almost sounded offended.

Cassius looked down and smiled nervously. "You'll see."

Vira nodded as she watched him walk out of his room. Now she was all alone, and her thoughts ran wild again. She took another sip of her ice water before being startled by a squawk from a bird that seemed to be flying around near the palace.

She set her glass aside as she got up to see what was going on. She opened up the tiny window as she peered outside. At first, the bird was no longer in sight. But the next second, another startling squawk sound caused her to jerk her head back from the window. She laid a hand on her chest. She could feel her beating heart. Finally, the bird came to the windowsill and parked itself on the ledge. It was clearly a pigeon now that Vira had gotten a better look at it.

"Hey there," she said jokingly as if it would respond.

As her heart rate slowed down, she stepped forward again, noticing the bird had a piece of rolled up paper in its mouth. She squinted her eyes in disbelief. She couldn't believe someone had actually sent her a letter. It seemed impossible. Better yet, she was surprised someone knew where she was. Half of her panicked from the thought of danger coming from reading it and the other half thought there was no way it could even be for her.

But Vira looked closer to the pigeon, and the piece of paper had a seal on it that was stamped with the letter *A*. Her eyes widened in great shock.

"Altha?" The name burst out of her in shock as if she had just made an appearance at the palace.

After all, it had to have been from her if it was from anyone back at the palace.

No more than a second went by when Vira took the note from the pigeon's mouth.

"Thank you," she said to the bird shortly before it took off.

Vira peeled off the seal and unrolled the paper. She leaned against the wall, eager to read what Altha had sent her.

Vira,

I miss you dearly, needless to say. I heard you've been detained, but by all means, I'm sure you're where you needed to be in order to survive if Maeryn handed you the news in time about death being in your future if you don't flee back to the Wintercastle Palace. If this note gets to you, it would mean a lot to me if you would write back. The peace in mind just to know you're alive would ease my pain. I've been worried sick about you.

- Altha

It sent a chill of relief down Vira's back to know her dearest friend didn't hate her. More so, that it didn't seem that Altha got in any trouble since nobody suspected her thankfully. The guilt faded and the fact that she now knew Altha didn't want to leave her behind created an ear to ear smile on Vira.

Right away, Vira knew she needed to write back to Altha. Altha didn't even know she was alive, and the least she could do was give her the news.

So Vira grabbed a notebook from Cassius' shelf of hundreds of books and tore out a blank page. She sat on the couch after picking up a quilted ink feather from the side table. She placed the paper on top of the book to write better, and began doing so.

Altha,

Surely, I'm alive, thanks for asking. Your consideration is dear to me. In fact, I'm more alive than I've ever been before. I made it back to the palace in the nick of time and as I dropped to the floor, Cassius had gotten to me fast enough to save me from what the venom was doing to my insides. He is a healer, just like you. An amazing one at that. He saved my life. And now I'm his queen, or soon to be. I miss you the most out of everything back home. Actually, you're the only thing I miss. Except now, this is my home, so I suppose you're the only thing I regret leaving behind in Siciland. Keep writing to me, as I miss you and would love hearing from you.

- Vira

One thing that struck Vira's memory as she wrote the letter was the fact that she still hadn't told Altha that Cassius killed Zereck's late mother a while back. Surely, it would be the right thing to do and she knew that, but now wasn't the time to do so. Vira imagined they'd never meet anyways. More so, there was no need to do so, as she imagined that she would only be able to communicate with Altha through letters from now on. It was a sad truth, but perhaps it was also for the better. With Zereck being a wolf shifter, Cassius may as well consider himself dead if he ever found out about it. More so, Cassius still didn't know Zereck and how he was the love of Vira's best friend's life. So it went all ways, really, since Zereck's mother attempted to kill Cassius, it was all even. Even if his mother was the only one who was dead now.

Vira opened up the window, then whistled with her two fingers to a pigeon that sat on a tree branch she could only see from a distance.

The pigeon turned its head, then flew to the window cill. After Vira rolled the paper up and tied a small piece of string around it, she handed it to the bird and he grabbed it with his mouth.

"Altha Blumen." Vira nodded to the bird. She hadn't ever sent a letter by pigeon before, so she had no clue if what she did was right. But she supposed she'd find out if she got another letter from Altha like she asked for in the letter. Supposedly, it was the same pigeon that had given her Altha's note in the first place, so there was a chance it would catch onto the trend.

As soon as the bird took off, Cassius entered the room again. Vira was somewhat startled by his sudden appearance, so she casually acted as if she was just looking out the window for fun.

"Queen, darling," he greeted.

Vira turned around to face him with a smile on her face. She didn't know why she all of a sudden got worried like she was hiding something or that she needed to hide the letter from Altha from him, but she tucked it in her dress pocket.

"Cass, hi." Her smile stayedon her face as she spoke.

"I've been working on something for you." He stepped closer towards her, extending an arm to her. "Come."

Vira took her arm in his. As they linked arms, he guided her down the hallway of the palace.

VIRA'S NEW ROOM

V ira was half excited and half confused, wondering where Cassius could possibly have been taking her now.

They stopped at the widest door in the hallway, reminiscent of the room Vira had back at Siciland palace.

"So how long have you been working on this?" Vira asked, breaking the silence between them the entire walk to the room.

Cassius smiled. It seemed like he was about to say something, then stopped. Instead, he answered by only using his other hand to twist the knob and open the door.

When it opened, Vira couldn't believe her eyes as they walked in together, still linked to each other.

"Cassius, it's gorgeous." She looked around in awe.

The lighting wasn't nearly as dim as the rest of the palace, thankfully. It was more of a sunset glow. Vira smiled at the fact that Cassius had thought of her and the abilities of his she didn't have that he did. She looked towards the far wall to see that it was filled with painting supplies, an easel and several canvases, and more paint than she had ever seen before. Then, a small door met her view. Vira walked over to it, then turned the knob. There stood a bathroom.

Vira looked back and chuckled. "You even thought of installing a toilet?" She was surprised to see a bathroom even more fancy than the one in her previous room. The golden detailing complimented the light gray painted walls perfectly.

"It took me long and hard to think of all of the things you'd need in here while you were still in the coma." He sounded like he would have blushed if he could.

"Ah," Vira nodded, looking up and down the bathroom, then walking out of it.

Immediately, she was met with a bed twice the size of the one back at Siciland. The pastel blue and deep red floral designs decorated it with golden tassels upon the shams to compliment.

She leaned her hand on the comforter and as she did, she laughed as it sunk in. Her laugh then rubbed off on Cassius.

"May I show you now..." He walked over to the part of the room Vira hadn't yet ventured. It was yet another door.

Without saying another word, Cassius opened the door. Vira walked closer to it, and all she could see were shades of deep red but mostly black.

"You'd only have one dress if I didn't find you any more." He waved his hand, motioning to them.

"They're..." Vira picked out one of the dresses and looked it up and down. "Beautiful." It surely was the truth. "I'll try one on later." She smiled.

The dress was far more comfortable than the itchy gown she had on. Vira could tell just by the touch. She'd be more than glad to never wear the dress she currently had on again.

"I'd love to see you in it." Cassius grinned, flaring a glimpse of his extended canines.

Vira set the dress back inside of the closet and sat on the bed.

"So, Cass," she started. He looked up at her in acknowledgement. "This is now my room," she concluded.

"Yes." he nodded his head.

"And your room is at the other end of the hall," she observed.

"Yes."

"So, we have separate rooms?" She almost sounded offended.

Perhaps Vira should have also considered the fact that she wouldn't even get dressed in front of him yet. Not at Siciland Palace, nor right here right now. But she knew that didn't equate to not sharing a room.

"That's the tradition, isn't it?" he asked.

Vira's heart went cold for a moment, upset by his passiveness.

"We're not the same king and queen everyone else has ever been, Cass," she argued. "We're Vira and Cassius, soon to be both Strike."

"Yes," he nodded. "But Vira, love, you realize there are two things that you aren't remembering now, right?"

Vira's eyebrows drew in together. "Obviously not."

"One, I don't sleep." He shook his head. "None of my monarchical family members slept because we were all vampires."

"So, what does that mean?" she asked.

"The queen had too many belongings to fit into the king's room, and vice versa. She was too valuable for her items to be held by someone else," he explained. "The tradition of the king and queen having separate rooms was started by your place, Siciland, and it's different here."

Vira nodded in realization, then felt foolish for sounding offended that he hadn't thought to join their rooms into one.

"But in case you're wondering, yes, I will be staying in here as you fall asleep tonight." He patted the bed as he sat down on it.

"Will you still be here as I wake up?" she asked, half as an inside joke they now had.

Cassius laughed softly and said, "Every morning for the rest of time."

Vira leaned into him and let their heads fall together. His skin was still as chilled as ever, but Vira still loved it.

"You know, I can't believe you chose me," he spoke softly.

Vira retracted from him and cocked her head. "Why on earth wouldn't I choose you?"

"Oh, you know, just, our circumstances, and the life it'll bring us," he said. "It still seems surreal I could be so lucky to love you."

"What do you mean by this?" Vira asked, eager for him to elaborate.

"Oh, you know, you left everyone behind for me, and you were so willing to help me even when you wanted to kill me."

"Best mistake I ever made." Vira's cheeks went rose colored as she smiled.

"You know, you are welcome any time if you'd like to change your mind, though, I'm not too sure I'd be okay with that now that I have a will to exist." He motioned to her, grazing the bottom of her chin with his finger.

Perhaps the enemy's side of them still stuck around to a degree.

"I'd never kill you. I could never do that to either of us." She shook her head.

"Well, the day may come where I will ask you to," he said, sounding serious.

Vira's eyes grew wide as she was struck with shock. "What?" she said a little too loud.

"It's what I meant by our circumstance." He had yet to elaborate even more.

"Cassius." Vira's heart began to pound. "When would the day come where I would have to kill you?"

Cassius' nerves looked to rise. It seemed like there was something Cassius knew that Vira didn't, and it alarmed her. "I'm a vampire and you're a sorcerer. We have different lives. I'll live near eternity and your life is only a prolonged one."

Vira's stomach went sour when she realized that he was right. She felt a fool for not realizing earlier that they'd be separated at some point and that, one day, their happily ever after would come to an end.

"You'd want to die, then, before I do?" she stuttered to speak as she couldn't catch her racing heart.

Cassius almost laughed before he said, "You are my only reason for existing. Most of the time, I was half debating whether I'd need the crown or not. But I'm glad I went for it. If I wouldn't have met you, I'd be dead by now."

"You wouldn't just want to find another queen or something?" she asked.

Cassius looked at Vira like she had just insulted him. "Vira, I could never find someone to replace you. You're a beautiful soul to me, the one thing us vampires lack. I couldn't leave you behind. I know if this was the other way around, I'd rather be decapitated and set on fire a hundred times before seeing you smile at the thought of another man."

Vira's heart went from ice cold to warm. She loved his words. And at that, she hated facing the fact that it would all have to come to an end. There wasn't enough time for everything to happen.

"Wow." She was taken aback.

"What is it, Vira?" He scooted closer to her, placing his hand on her shoulder and leaning into her in confort.

"I guess I just never realized this would all come to an end. I thought we'd be together for eternity. I long for that."

Without another word, Cassius rested his head upon her face in comfort, allowing her to phase out the pain in the moment.

After seconds of stillness, he then retracted his head from her and said, "You're starving."

Vira nodded. "You're right. I haven't eaten."

"Let's head down to the table. I've collected some food for you as well while you were asleep."

Vira touched her stomach. It was nearly numb with how empty it was.

"It'll lighten the mood, make you feel better. Besides, we've got lots to discuss about your crowning ceremony, soon-to-be queen," he said with a smile as he stood up.

He held an arm out to her again, then she took it, already feeling better about their conversation from earlier and the realization that felt like a sneak attack.

ACKNOWLEDGEMENTS

First, I would like to thank all of my readers out there. You guys allow me to do what I love every day. In particular, I would like to thank my beta readers. I am able to make my books better one by one, because of you guys. And for that, I just have to give you credit on any and all success I have had within my author journey.

I would also like to thank everyone in my life. My family members and my closest friends, you guys do it all. You support me, you love me and you make me happy. I couldn't do it without you guys either.

I would also love to thank all of my favorite authors who have only continued to inspire me to keep doing what I love and to turn away from any and all discouragement. They made me believe I could do it, because they surely did.

Last, I would also like to thank everyone who has played a part in materializing this book. I would like to thank my cover designer, Asqa and my editor, Daniela. They were as passionate about this project as I was, and it means a lot to have people who want to work for me and support me, going beyond just doing their job.

Milton Keynes UK
Ingram Content Group UK Ltd.
UKHW011952210823
427215UK00004B/348